Sworn Jury

Other books by John D. Mills:

Reasonable and Necessary
The Manatee Murders
The Objector
The Trophy Wife Divorce
The Hooker, the Dancer and the Nun

Sworn Jury

by

John D. Mills

www.PonoPubs.com

Library of Congress Control Number: TBA

ISBN -13: 978-1522894308
ISBN -10: 1522894306

Printed in the United States Second Edition
Third Printing, October 2019

Editor: Megan Parker, Calliope & Quill Layout and editing: Inge Heyer

Pono Publishing Laramie, Wyoming Hilo, Hawai`i

www.PonoPubs.com

Acknowledgements

I am grateful to the following people who read my origi- nal manuscript and offered ideas for improvement:

Amy Anthony
Doug Wilkinson
Bruce Oliphant
Gail Lawson
John Shearer
Terri Hendricks
Lisa Skinner
Judge Isaac Anderson
Megan Parker
Stephanie J. Slater
Timothy F. Slater
Inge Heyer

Chapter 1

Monday afternoon, 2:02 p.m.

"Ladies and gentlemen of the jury, the State of Florida thanks you for your jury service. This will be a week-long murder trial, maybe more, depending how things develop. But, in any event, your service is appreciated by the State Attorney's Office."

Brian Spere, the prosecutor, remembering his mentor's training, hesitated three seconds and slowly looked all twelve members of the jury in the eye. He lowered his voice and continued in a somber tone, "The body was found in the driver's seat of a 1919 Model T Ford located in the garage of the historic Edison Estate."

Spere waited for the shock to fall off the faces of the jurors. Yes, they were the jury on the biggest case to ever be tried in Ft. Myers. Spere waited until one of the jurors leaned forward in anticipation, and he continued, "One of the main- tenance workers entered the garage of the historic Edison Estate on the foggy morning of January 18th of this year to polish Mr. Edison's original Model T before the tours started at nine o'clock. He will never forget the nude, bloody body he saw tied to the driver's seat with a blue rope and the hands fastened to the wheel with a yellow bungee cord. There were two bullet holes in his chest and his head was slumped over to his right side, with the eyes still open. The night before, the Edison Home had their annual black tie fundraiser and the victim had attended, but never left."

Ray Harrison, the defense attorney, had prepared his

cli- ent, Dallas Kelley, for this moment. He counseled him to not look away when the jury turned and stared at him when the gruesome details of the murder came out during the prosecu- tion's opening statement. He knew the jury would look at the accused and silently ask themselves, "*How could he do that?*"

When Dallas returned the stares of the jury, he never flinched. He even managed a slight smile towards juror num- ber three, a recently divorced mother of three teenage boys. Ray looked down at his yellow pad and doodled, chuckling to himself over his client's ego. The man was on trial for his life and he was hitting on women. Or was he trying to charm one of his jurors? Ray thought about Dallas's background as a mover and shaker in real estate circles and decided he was probably multi-tasking, playing both angles and to see how it developed.

The jury looked away from Dallas and focused back on Spere as he slowly and methodically went through a preview of the evidence. Ray's adrenaline was pumping through his body, his eyes scanning the jury to see how they were react- ing to the prosecutor's opening statement while listening intently. There were no eye witnesses that observed Dallas shooting his long-time lawyer, Bryce Cervante, but there was a substantial amount of circumstantial evidence. The State had a rock-solid motive because Dallas had recently spent $500,000 dollars in attorney fees to Cervante for a zoning hearing on a failed real estate development. Cervante had a conflict of interest he hid from Dallas, which was later discovered, and Dallas blamed Cervante for the denial of his zoning variance and lost money on fees. Ray knew he faced an uphill battle.

** ** ** ** ** **

"Give me a Dewars and water, please," Ray told the waitress at the Veranda. She smiled and walked through the happy hour crowd toward the bar. Ray liked the Veranda for happy hour after court because it was one block from the courthouse, so he didn't have to fight rush hour traffic. His clients would never like the fact that he socialized with prosecutors, cops, and probation officers there, so he nicknamed it 'Courtroom V.' When leaving court, Ray could say to the rival prosecutor, "I'll see you later in Courtroom V," without upsetting his clients.

The Veranda was two old antebellum mansions that had been moved together and converted to a restaurant and piano bar. They were once on the front edge of an orange grove.

After World War I, the grove was sold and developed. When entering the restaurant, it was like stepping back in time to the town's southern roots. The high wooden walls were covered with historical black and white photographs that document the hunting, fishing, and agriculture of a different era in Ft. Myers. The entire back wall was covered with large windows and French doors, which opened onto a red brick patio, surrounded by native vegetation and areca palms. A goldfish pond in the rear of the patio was popular with children.

The waitress returned with Ray's drink and he took a quick belt. The first taste of scotch always made his taste buds shiver, but as it went down his belly welcomed back a familiar friend. Ray had just finished the first day of the trial twenty minutes before and he was glad to be away from the courtroom, the media, and his client.

His adrenaline had been pumping since 9:00 a.m. when

jury selection began. Judge Stalman pushed everyone and didn't adjourn for lunch until the jury was picked at 1:00 p.m. After a lunch break, the prosecutor's opening statement lasted for forty-five minutes and Ray's opening statement had only lasted twenty minutes, where he blamed an unnamed scorned woman for the murder. Ray's investigator had found three current girlfriends of the victim that were
attending the fundraiser. Ray was always amused with TV shows and movies depicting the defense team with an airtight alibi and bumbling state's witnesses that always said the right things to help the defense.

In reality, trials were decided on whether jurors liked witnesses. If a jury didn't like a witness, they wouldn't believe what she had to say. Ray always sat back in his chair and listened carefully to what the witness said and tried to find inconsistencies with any prior statements. It was one of his specialties on cross-examination; he methodically confronted the witness with these inconsistencies. When the witness was confronted with her different details, it made the witness mad, and therefore, unlikable to the jury. Ray had made a good living over the past twenty years making witnesses unlikable.

After opening statements were over, Judge Stalman dismissed the jury for the day. He and the lawyers stayed and discussed his proposed jury instructions until 5:30 p.m. Ray was ready for a drink when he finally made it to the Veranda.

Ray took another drink of scotch and started to relax. He was sitting at a corner table, between a towering wine rack on one wall and an oversized fireplace on the other. The walls were painted a cream color that contrasted with the dark wood of the fireplace, wine rack, and tables. A
4

thick, hunter green carpet was on the floor in the bar and seating area. The old hardwood floor was still showcased in the hall-way to the serving area and kitchen.

Ray was waiting for his girlfriend, Amber Fazig, to finish work and join him. It was not unusual for a divorced lawyer to meet his girlfriend for happy hour and dinner at the Veranda after work. What was unusual about the situation was Amber was a TV reporter covering Ray's murder trial.

Amber was doing a live report from the front of the courthouse for the six o'clock news. She told Ray she would join him after she finished.

Ray drained his glass and signaled to the waitress for a second drink. He looked at his watch and estimated he had five to ten minutes before Amber showed up. He remembered back six months when he'd first met her. He'd just won an acquittal for his stockbroker client accused of securities fraud. Ray had convinced the jury the defendant hadn't intentionally misled investors in a failed "dot-com" business. He successfully argued the "dot-com" executives had lied to his client about the profitability of the business, making their greed the focus of the trial, and the executives very unlikable in the process.

After the verdict, Ray was on the steps of the federal courthouse fielding questions from reporters. From his left he heard a woman's voice shout, "How does it feel to get a con man off when he lost the life savings of teachers, preachers, and disabled people?"

Ray focused on a petite blonde with ocean blue eyes, jamming a microphone toward him. She was a new reporter looking for a good quote—nailing better ratings always meant getting a better job. He took a deep breath, stared into her eyes and said, "I'll answer that question if you'll answer mine first. Don't you think Jesus could've used a good criminal defense lawyer before they executed him?"

All of the camera men from the other TV stations turned their cameras toward Amber. She felt her face flush as she tried to think of an answer. She'd never been asked an unanswerable question before with cameras turned on her and bright lights shining in her eyes. She couldn't say anything and Ray sensed the other TV stations had their sound bite for the story. He said goodbye to everyone and said he was going to celebrate with his client. Ray was right about his sound bite—the other TV stations loved that a rival reporter was embarrassed and that a lawyer was bold enough to compare his lucky client to Jesus.

The next day Amber called his office and asked for an interview about the case because her bosses had threatened to fire her over her screw-up. She begged for an exclusive interview to save her job. Ray remembered the blonde hair and blue eyes of the pretty young reporter and quickly agreed to an interview at his office. Ray did an extended interview and gave her some good insights for her story. He asked her out the next day, and they'd been dating since then.

Ray was looking out at the courtyard, watching palms sway in the wind and daydreaming about his case. It was late summer, and Ray could feel the humidity rise as the clouds thickened for the normal late afternoon rain. Over the happy hour crowd noise, he heard one guy at the piano bar say to a buddy in a loud whisper, "Look at that."

Ray looked over toward the door because he was sure that Amber had just made her entrance. He guessed correctly and watched as she looked around, letting her eyes adjust to the lower light of the bar. Amber was used to men staring at her and smiled politely. Her boss had taught her you never knew where the next news tip was coming from or whom you would interview next. She had learned men gave more candid interviews if they thought they had a chance with her.

As Amber approached, Ray stood up and pulled out her chair. All of the other men watched as she sat down with Ray, disappointed she wasn't there alone. She gave Ray a cheek kiss and a squeeze on his arm when he leaned into her. She sat down and took a deep breath. "What a day. I need a drink."

Ray sat back down. "Tell me about it."

The waitress came to the table and Amber ordered a Cosmopolitan. After the waitress left, she continued, "Well, this morning I had to go down to the beach to cover a group of beached dolphins. We did a live shot for the noon news at the beach pier. They then sent me down to Bonita to cover a dedication of the new library. After that, I had to come back

downtown for the six o'clock live shot from the courthouse about your trial."

Amber leaned back into her comfortable wing back chair, covered with burgundy leather, and sighed. Ray smiled and said in his best deadpan voice, "I've been a little busy too."

Amber leaned forward as she said, "Tell me about the trial. Give me some stuff I can use in tomorrow's report."

The waitress brought Amber her drink and she took a quick sip. She continued, "Come on, tell me the inside story."

Ray leaned back in his chair and smiled, "Well, we've got a sworn jury so all bets are off. It's put up or shut up time."

Amber asked, "I've never understood what's so

important about the jury being sworn."

Ray answered with a mischievous smile, "Once the jury is sworn, jeopardy attaches to the case, so if the prosecutor makes a mistake and the trial doesn't go the way the State wants it to, the defendant can't be retried a second time.

That's called double jeopardy. For instance, if O.J. Simpson was interviewed by Barbara Walters and he said, 'I really did kill my wife,' he can't be retried for the same crime twice."

Amber rolled her eyes and said, "Yeah, yeah. But that's an extreme case, and stuff like that rarely happens." Ray snickered and looked around to make sure there wasn't anyone from the State Attorney's Office close by and asked, "Have you ever heard of the 'village idiot' story from LaBelle?"
Amber shook her head.

Ray continued, "There was this prosecutor in LaBelle named Alfred Woodson. He wasn't the brightest guy in the world, but he was loyal, so his bosses gave him the job as administrative attorney in LaBelle. It's a small farming city on the east side of the circuit with not too much serious crime. So they figured he couldn't screw things up too bad. Boy, were they wrong!

"After a couple of years being out of the courtroom, he decided he was going to try a murder case. Well, during opening statements, after the jury was sworn, he starts objecting to the defense's opening statements. The judge overrules him on five different occasions. Well, ole Alfred stands up at the end of the defense's opening statement and says, 'Your Honor, the defense lawyer misrepresented the facts to the jury. I move for a mistrial.' The judge looks at him in disbelief, and after a few seconds of thought says,
8

'Mr. Woodson, I'm going to give you exactly what you asked for. Motion granted.'"

Ray took a drink and Amber asked, "So what's so bad about that? Lawyers call each other names all the time."

Ray shook his head, "Yeah, but the State asked for a mistrial. Because it was the State's request, the defendant can't be retried for the same crime. The defendant got away with murder and the judge gave Alfred the nickname of 'village idiot.'"

Amber asked, "Did he get fired?"

Ray laughed and continued, "Not until two years later. He fucked up another murder trial and another defendant walked."

"You've got to be kidding me!"

"No, I'm not," Ray took a hit of his drink, sat back in his chair, and continued, "Alfred was embarrassed after the first murder trial and stayed out of the courtroom for two years, but his pride got the best of him. He got tired of people telling the village idiot story, so he waited until a perfect murder case came along that was impossible to lose. At least until Alfred got involved.

"The facts of the case were two business partners got into an argument over money and one shot the other. The body was dumped in a lake and surfaced a few days later. The gun was found in a dumpster behind the store and the partner's fingerprints were on the gun. The ballistics expert matched the bullet in the body to being fired from the gun with the partner's fingerprints on it. The local banker testified about the business disputes between the two, so the jury had a motive to explain the shooting.

"The problem came in the chain of custody of the gun. While the gun was in custody of the sheriff's department, an evidence locker was dropped on it and left a big scratch on the gun. No one at the State Attorney's office knew about the new scratch. When the cop who collected the gun from the dumpster was on the stand, Alfred asked him, 'Is this gun in the same condition as when you found it?' and the honest cop answered, 'No.'

"Alfred asked to have the gun entered into evidence, the defense lawyer objected and the judge sustained his objection. Alfred never could get the gun into evidence and therefore, without the gun in evidence, the expert could not match up the bullets or the fingerprints of the defendant. Because he couldn't get the gun in evidence, the defendant walked."

Amber crinkled her eyes. "That doesn't seem fair."

Ray nodded and said, "You're right. If Alfred had just asked the witness, 'Is this gun in *substantially* the same condition as when you found it?' then the witness could've answered, 'Yes, it's in the same condition except for the scratch on the side.' The experts could've been asked if that scratch made a difference in their opinion, and they would've said no. Every first-year law student knows how to ask the right questions. But not the village idiot. They finally fired him after that."

Amber took another sip of her drink and thought about the village idiot. She asked, "Why should the victim's family be penalized because of an incompetent prosecutor?"

"That's the way the game's played. Once the jury is sworn, jeopardy attaches and the defendant can't be tried twice for the same crime. It's in our constitution."

Amber wasn't satisfied and asked, "Are there any other times you've known someone to get off because of double jeopardy?"

Ray nodded, "When I first started out, there was this

big armed robbery trial. A drug dealer was robbed at gun point, and the defendant hoped the drug dealer wouldn't report it. He was wrong. At trial, the victim was asked, 'Do you see the man in court who robbed you?' The victim answered, 'I'm not sure. It could be the defendant, but he has a twin, and the only way I can tell them apart is that one of them has a barbed wire tattoo on his right arm. The one with the tattoo is the one who robbed me.'

"Everyone in the courtroom looked at the defendant, and he slowly rolled up his right sleeve to show no tattoos. The witness blurts out, 'No, it's not him.' There was one other witness that identified the defendant as the robber, but the jury wasn't convinced, and they came back with a not guilty verdict. After the trial, a reporter asked the defendant about the verdict when he was leaving the courthouse, and the defendant laughed. He rolled up his left sleeve to show a barb wire tattoo. The victim screwed up on which arm had the tattoo, but he couldn't be retried because of double jeopardy."

Amber finished her drink and motioned to the waitress for another. She asked, "Any other double jeopardy stories?"

Ray sighed. "An all too common situation is domestic violence cases. After the man is arrested, he calls up his wife and apologizes and swears it'll never happen again. The wife takes him back and stops cooperating with the prosecutors. Months later on the trial day, the jury is sworn and she doesn't show up to testify. The case is dismissed because of lack of evidence. A week later the same problems start, and she kicks the husband out of the house. She frantically calls up the prosecutor and wants to redo the criminal case. Unfortunately, the prosecutor's hands are tied because of the double jeopardy issue and they can't do the case a second time."

Amber crossed her arms and frowned. "Other than domestic violence cases, when does double jeopardy become a problem?"

"Well, one of the most common screw-ups is the charging document, called the information. It has to allege the date of the crime, the type of crime, and the name of the defendant. Every once in a while there is a typo on the date of the crime, and the prosecutor doesn't catch it before trial. At the end of the trial, the defense lawyer argues to the judge that all of the events testified to at trial occurred on March 3rd of the current year, but the information alleges all of the events occurred on March 3rd of the prior year. The judge looks menacingly at the prosecutor, and growls, 'Case dismissed.'"

Amber shook her head in disgust. She looked at Ray and asked, "How many cases have you won that way?"

Ray drained his glass as he thought of his answer. "Probably a dozen over the past twenty years."

Chapter 2

Monday evening, 7:30 p.m.

The waitress asked, "Would you like some dessert?" Ray looked over at Amber, "How about it?" Amber's eyes lit up. "I'll have the crème brûlée."

Ray tapped his empty drink glass and said, "I'll have a liquid dessert."

As the waitress walked away, Amber leaned forward and touched Ray's arm. "Give me some dirt on the victim. I need a good tip so I can get the lead story on the noon report, and that way they'll keep me on the trial all week. I like watching you in trial; it's fun to watch you weave your theory into your questions—it drives the prosecutors crazy."

Ray also liked it when Amber covered his trials. It gave him extra confidence knowing he spent the night with the woman every man in the courthouse lusted for. He knew it was a juvenile reason that he would never reveal to anyone. But he still liked it.

The regular pianist at the Veranda, Lila, had started playing easy listening music. Everyone in the restaurant and bar enjoyed the perfectly played songs as she joyfully entertained. A few of the regulars moved from their tables to the piano bar to get closer to the musical treat.

Ray leaned back and stretched his arms, clasping his hands behind his head. "Bryce Cervante—what an interesting resume. After he graduated from law school at the University of Florida, he moved back here to his hometown and started a real estate practice. He did very well for himself practicing law, but he made his real money putting together real estate trusts that bought and sold large tracts of land."

Amber inched forward in her chair and asked, "So how'd he make so much money on these real estate trusts?"

"He'd sell ten percent interests to doctors, lawyers, dentists, and anybody that had a spare $100,000 to invest. The deal was that he sold ninety percent of the trust to other people and he kept ten percent of the trust as his fee for being the organizer. Think about it; he'd get $900,000 of other people's money and buy land. Say two years later, the land sold for three million. His fee would be $300,000 and he never put up one cent of his own money.

Amber whistled. "That's a nice chunk of change."

Ray nodded. "He did very well over the years and people were lining up to invest money with him. He used his hometown connections to sniff out good real estate deals and to influence his boyhood friends on the county commission to give him favorable zoning variances on property his trusts purchased. He always made sure brown bags of cash were left at the right houses at Christmas. It was enough to make Santa blush."

Amber cocked her head to one side and asked, "How do you know all of this?"

Ray smiled. "I have a very good investigator who's a fifth-generation native. He's an ex-cop with Irish bloodlines and he drinks in every bar in town."

The waitress brought their desserts and both of their taste buds went into overdrive. After a swallow of scotch Ray continued, "Well, ya'll already reported about his womanizing ways. His wife divorced him five years ago because his affairs were the worst kept secrets in town. She got the house and half of the investments. I guess the alimony and child support will end, but at least his three kids should get a nice inheritance."

Amber shook her head. "That's old news. Give me something fresh that I can confirm."

Ray immediately thought about his connection to the victim: his ex-wife, Helen, was married to Cervante's former law partner, Larry Alston. The two law partners had a very public breakup of their firm two years before because of Cervante's affair with Helen. None of the TV stations or newspapers had reported this connection to Ray, and he certainly wasn't going to divulge it to his pit-bull reporter girlfriend. Ray had no delusions about his girlfriend's priorities.

Ray smiled and leaned forward. "I've got a juicy tidbit for you that you can confirm. And it'll give your viewers a good insight into the type of lawyer Bryce Cervante was."

Amber pushed the last bit of the crème brûlée on her spoon as she lowered her voice. "Do tell."

Ray cleared his throat. "You know where the Wal-Mart warehouse is out on Metro parkway, by the railroad tracks?"

"Yeah, what about it?"

"Twenty years ago, Bryce represented the trust that owned the land, and Wal-Mart wanted to buy it. They negotiated back and forth for forty acres of land that abutted Metro and the rail line. As you can imagine, the lawyer representing Wal-Mart and Bryce negotiated back and forth, in writing, with all the legal description of the property listed. They made dozens of offers and counter offers. They finally agreed to sell the property to Wal-Mart for ten million.

"A year later, when Wal-Mart was finishing up construction of their warehouse, Bryce puts up a fence between the warehouse and the railroad tracks. He sends Wal-Mart a letter and shows them copies of all the different offers and counter offers between him and their attorney. Bryce had pulled a fast one. In his last counter-offer to Wal-Mart, he changed the legal description of the tract of land to leave out a fifty foot strip of land between the railroad tracks and the other property. Wal-Mart had agreed to pay ten million for the property minus the fifty foot strip.

"Wal-Mart was screwed because they needed this fifty foot strip to access the railway. They ended up paying twelve million for this fifty foot strip, fired their attorney, and sued him for malpractice. All of what I told you is public record over in the clerk's office. You've got your confirmation and an exclusive story for the noon news."

Amber smiled. "Now that's a good story. My producer will be so excited to break the story that he'll let me cherry pick the good leads for the next month."

Lila was playing Billy Joel's "Piano Man" as the regulars sang along. Ray and Amber sat and enjoyed the show as they finished their desserts. After the song was over, the diners clapped for their joint efforts. Amber moved her chair back and stood up. "I need to go to the little girl's room. I'll be right back."

As Ray enjoyed the view of Amber walking away, his thoughts drifted back to the trial. The State's theory of the case was that his client, Dallas Kelley, was furious with Cervante because of a failed development where Cervante had represented Dallas and his investors. There was a zoning variance hearing about some environmentally sensitive property Dallas was trying to get rezoned for development. Dallas had paid a $500,000 fee to Cervante to get the commissioners to grant a zoning variance.

Cervante hadn't disclosed that he was a ten percent

owner of a trust that owned land next to the property Dallas owned. Cervante was also trying to get a variance for this property for development. Both properties were equally questionable for development because of the aquifer underneath both properties, which supplied the city's drinking water. Coincidentally, the zoning hearing for both properties was held on the same day.

Cervante paid $300,000 of his investor's money to an environmental consulting firm to give testimony about the safety of his development. At the zoning hearing, the consultant pointed to the potential development of Dallas's property as the real danger to the underground aquifer. Dallas sat in amazement in the audience area and squirmed through the damning testimony. After the consultant's testimony, the county commission granted a variance to Cervante's property and denied it to Dallas's.

Dallas stood up and cursed the commissioners before he stormed out of the meeting chambers. Cervante's property quadrupled in value, and Dallas's property became worthless. Cervante hadn't told Dallas ahead of time about the consultant that was going to torpedo his development. Dallas was furious his attorney was representing a competing development, whose consultant had trashed his development, and that he hadn't been told about it ahead of time so he could have hired a different expert to rebut the claim of damage.

The newspaper had reported about the testimony of the consultant helping one development and dooming the other. The following weekend, Dallas was playing golf with one of the trust investors in Cervante's development. He told Dallas that Cervante was a ten percent owner of the successful development, in addition to being their attorney. Dallas went berserk. He drove his BMW to Cervante's office and broke all of the windows with his 9 iron. The police arrested Dallas for vandalism, and the newspaper blew the story up all over the front page.

Unfortunately for Dallas, Cervante was murdered a week later at the Edison Home during the annual fundraiser for the Edison Historical Society. It was a black tie event attended by 500 of the patrons of the Edison Historical Society. The morning after the fundraiser, Cervante's nude body was found tied up in the 1919 Model T Ford in the garage of the Edison Home. There were two bullet holes through Cervante's heart and two .22 caliber bullets were found lodged in the driver's seat of the car.

The police interviewed a number of people at the fundraiser, and they all reported an argument between Dallas and Cervante at the bar, located underneath the giant banyan tree by the gift shop. Dallas shoved Cervante and they had to be separated before the fists started flying. An off-duty police officer, working the security detail, had escorted Dallas to his car. As Dallas was getting into his BMW, he yelled to the officer, "Tell that cocksucker I'm not done with him."

After the body was found, the police went to Dallas's house with a search warrant and found a .22 caliber semiautomatic under his BMW's driver's seat. There were no fingerprints on the gun, but blood spatter was found inside the barrel, indicating the gun was pressed to the skin when fired. The ballistic tests matched the gun to the bullets found inside the driver's seat of the Model T. Dallas was arrested and held with no bond.

Ray had a simple but powerful theory—it was a setup. Everyone around town knew about the feud between Dallas and Cervante. Hundreds of people witnessed the pushing scene at the fundraiser, and Cervante was liked by a few and hated by many. There were no eyewitnesses to the shooting and no physical evidence, other than the gun found in Dallas's car. Three of Cervante's current girlfriends were at the fundraiser, and Ray suggested one of them became angry with Cervante and shot him in a jealous rage. The real shooter killed Cervante and planted the gun in Dallas's car, knowing he would be the first person police suspected.

** ** ** ** **

Amber came back from the bathroom and moved her chair closer to Ray. She leaned toward Ray, and he caught a whiff of her freshly applied perfume as she whispered, "What are you thinking about?"

"Oh, I was just thinking about the case. We've got a lot of work ahead of us tomorrow."

Amber repositioned herself in her chair and leaned back, crossing her legs. Ray noticed that she had unbuttoned an additional button on her blouse. Amber said, "I've got a full plate myself. Work has been very stressful lately because they never replaced that pretty-boy reporter that quit last month to go work in Miami. The rest of us are picking up his workload."

Amber smiled at Ray and lowered her voice, "I need some stress relief."

Ray decided to play the straight man, "I've got some valium at my house."

Amber leaned forward, showing her ample cleavage, "I don't do valium; I do penises—they're cheaper and much more dependable."

Chapter 3

The alarm clock's music woke Ray and he rolled over, hitting the snooze button with his outstretched hand. He rolled back into the middle of his king-sized bed, snuggled up to Amber, and pulled the goose-down comforter up over his shoulders. Amber leaned back into Ray until their skin touched each other from head to foot. She let out a quiet sigh and drifted back to sleep. Ray adjusted his head on his pillow and was slowly drifting back to semi-unconsciousness when his second alarm clock went off.

Ray's second alarm clock was across the room on his dresser. It was battery-operated and obnoxiously loud with a steady pattern of buzzing. Ray jumped out of the warm bed and walked across the cool wood floor and turned off the alarm. Ray had been late to court before when his power had gone out. He could also ignore the music from the alarm clock next to his bed when he'd had a rough night of drinking. He learned the hard way to always set the second battery-operated alarm clock on days he had to be in court.

He was now chilled, wide awake, and out of bed. He grabbed his robe and stepped into his slippers as he heard his dog scratching on his bedroom door. Ray's dog was a Jack Russell, appropriately named Caesar because he ruled the household. Ray picked up Caesar when his wife left him three years before. Ray had channeled his loneliness on Caesar as a puppy, and the dog had learned to expect Ray's full attention. Caesar normally enjoyed a spot on the bed

21

with Ray, and he didn't like it when he was locked out of the bedroom when Amber stayed over.

Ray opened the door, and Caesar started yelping happily and jumping on Ray's leg. As Ray reached down and petted Caesar, he heard Amber groan and pull the comforter over her head. Ray snorted at Amber's antics and walked toward the front door to let out Caesar. He remembered the pet store owner's sales pitch when he was looking at Caesar: *"Dogs are the only love money can buy. They don't care when you get home, what you've been doing or who you've been with. They're always glad to see you."*

As Ray walked to the end of his driveway to get the morning paper, Caesar sniffed around the yard for an appropriate place for his business. The sun was just breaking the horizon of a clear sky. Ray could feel the heavy humidity and wondered if the normal afternoon rains might come early. Ray picked up the paper and headed back to the front door as Caesar narrowed his search. Ray stood on the front porch waiting for Caesar as he opened the paper. He moved underneath the front porch light as he looked at the paper's headlines. In bold letters, he read the headline, KILLER LAWYER DEFENDS ACCUSED KILLER.

Ray felt his face redden as he read the article, detailing how two years before he killed a man in self-defense and then was sued for wrongful death. Two years before, Ray picked up his daughters, Beth and Julie, from his ex-wife's house for their normal Tuesday night dinner. They always had dinner at an Italian joint on the south side of town, one of the girls' favorite restaurants. Afterward, as they approached Ray's car, in the rear of the parking lot, a man in dark clothes jumped out from behind a bush. He pulled a revolver and said very quietly, "Shut up, and no one will
22

get hurt."

The girls immediately screamed and started crying. The robber pointed the revolver at the girls and hissed, "Shut-up, or I'll shoot."

They latched on to each other and kept crying hysterically. Ray looked back at the robber and saw the veins popping out on his muscular neck. He knew from experience that most murder victims from robberies gone bad were panicking victims unnerving the desperate robbers. He quickly said in a calm voice, "Girls, get in the back seat and be quiet."

Ray looked at the robber. "I'm reaching into my pocket to get my keys."

The man nodded.

Ray reached into his pocket and pulled out his remote control key ring and unlocked the doors to his Lexus. The girls looked at Ray questionably and he said firmly, "Get in the car, and shut the door."

After the girls got in the car, Ray locked it with the remote. Then he turned and looked at the man in the dark clothes with oily hair and a week-old beard. He was at least four inches taller than Ray, outweighed him by fifty pounds, and appeared to be fifteen years younger. Ray said quietly, "I've got some cash in my wallet, and you can have my Rolex. I'm going to reach for my wallet now, O.K.?"

The man's eyes widened and he said forcefully, "I don't want your money. Give me your keys."

Ray suddenly realized this was a much more dangerous situation. This was not a random robbery; a predator had picked his daughters out for his sick fantasies, and Ray was going to be the first one killed. Ray stared at the revolver and quickly thought of all available options. He pressed the panic button on his remote control and the car alarm went off. The man instinctively turned his head toward the piercing sound, and Ray lunged forward. As he grabbed the revolver and pushed up, it fired and the bullet ripped into Ray's left shoulder.

The sound of the shot was deafening and the shoulder pain was excruciating, but the adrenaline flowed quickly through Ray's veins. Ray and the man fell to the ground with both of them wrestling for the revolver. As Ray and the man struggled for the gun, they were face to face and Ray could smell stale garlic coming from the man's mouth. Ray could hear his girls screaming for help from the Lexus. He felt himself losing the battle over the gun, and he imagined the man raping his daughters after he was killed. He jerked his head forward and bit down on the man's nose. He continued biting down and shaking his head until the man's nose was ripped from his face with the sound of crunched cartilage and a spray of blood.

As the man screamed out in pain, he let go of the gun. Ray gripped the gun and rolled to one side, looking over his shoulder at the man. He turned and fired three shots at the man, hitting him twice in the left leg and once in the hip.

The man screamed in agony and his girls were quiet as they stared at their father with the gun. Ray stood up and walked over to the fallen man, spitting his nose out. The man was holding his face, where his nose used to be, and pleaded, "Call an ambulance, I need help."

Ray realized the wounds were not life threatening and he started thinking. He knew how this worked, and he felt sick as he imagined the court case. He had represented a child rapist in the past and had learned their thought process about trials. When the rapist was arrested, he gave

24

a full confession to the police. The plea offer was only fifteen years in prison because the victim's family didn't want to put her through the ordeal of testifying at trial. The defendant refused the plea offer, knowing he could get life in prison if convicted. When Ray asked him why, he looked at Ray and smiled strangely. He said quietly, "I want to see the girl one more time in court."

The jury convicted the rapist and the judge sentenced him to life in prison, without a chance of parole. In the holding cell after sentencing, Ray had asked him if it was worth it. The defendant got that same sick smile on his face and just nodded.

Ray looked over at his girls in the car and their wide open eyes, their faces flushed with fear. He looked back down at the sicko pleading for an ambulance. It was easy to fire the two remaining bullets into the man's brain. No way were his daughters going to have to go to court and relive this night.

** ** ** ** **

Ray shook his head and went back inside his house and tossed the paper on the dining room table. Caesar ran into Ray's bedroom and jumped into bed with Amber and crawled under the covers, putting his cold nose on her feet. Ray could hear her cursing as he started the coffee and laughed to himself because Caesar always showed his displeasure of being evicted from the bed by Amber. He turned his TV on and switched to the local morning news. He sat down and read the follow-up article on page three about his legal problems after the shooting.

Two other patrons of the Italian restaurant had come

outside just before the first shots. They called 911 on their cell phone and watched what happened in the rear of the parking lot. They later told the police there were three shots in the beginning and then about thirty seconds went by before the remaining shots were fired. The police interviewed Ray, and he told them he felt light-headed from the loss of blood and he was scared the man was going to harm his children. He fired the remaining shots so they would be protected because he thought he was going to pass out. He lied and said he didn't remember where he pointed the gun; he just remembered pulling the trigger and emptying the gun before he sat down on the pavement and waited for the police. Ray felt completely justified about his lie; in fact, he was proud of it, even though he never admitted the truth to anyone.

No criminal charges were filed, but the widow of the dead man sued Ray for wrongful death. The widow's attorney called a press conference and labeled Ray a "killer lawyer." The phrase stuck, and the media used it every time they did a follow-up report. Ultimately, a judge dismissed the civil lawsuit against Ray, but it was a very painful public flogging. Even so, Ray became a bit of a celebrity after the nonstop reports of the shooting and the civil suit. Because of the publicity his practice flourished, but he never took a rape case after that.

Ray lived in a fifty-year-old ranch-styled house, and he had a large fenced-in back yard with a big oak tree in the middle. He built a tree house in it for his girls, and they customized it by painting it pink. He was constantly doing renovations and repairs so his handyman was on his speed dial. His favorite thing about the house was that it was ten minutes from his office.

In the kitchen, Ray got up and walked over to the

coffee pot and poured two cups of coffee. He walked into his bedroom with the two cups and saw Amber buttoning her blouse. He offered her a cup, and she waived it off as she grunted, "No."

Ray put her cup on the dresser and sat down on the edge of his bed. He took a sip of the steaming coffee and looked over at Amber straightening her skirt and blouse. Ray could tell Amber was irritated about something, but he wasn't sure what, and frankly, he didn't care. He had a murder trial that morning, and he had plenty of more important things to do than try to figure out why his moody, twenty-eight-year-old girlfriend was unhappy.

Amber opened her purse and attempted to brush her hair. She looked into the mirror but gave up after a couple of passes through the matted mess. Ray looked up at her and asked in a gentle voice, "Did you sleep well?" Amber looked over at Ray as she said gruffly, "Well, I did until about four in the morning. And then you started talking in your sleep about your ex-wife and her damn hair," Amber put her hands on her hips, "What is it about her rubbing you with her hair?"

Ray looked down and mumbled, "I'm sorry." Amber shook her head. "Whatever. I've got to go."

Amber stomped out of the bedroom and slammed the door. A two-foot piece of plaster fell off the bedroom wall and hit next to Caesar. He yelped as he instinctively jumped away. He looked at Ray with the look that said *I know it's her fault*. After Amber got through the front door, she slammed it even louder. Caesar barked and ran toward the door. Ray made a mental note to call his handyman.

Caesar jumped up on the bed and lay down next to him, resting his head on Ray's right thigh as Ray mentally replayed his first meeting with his ex-wife for the

27

hundredth time. Ray scratched Caesar behind his ears gently as he felt a headache forming. Ray took another sip of the coffee as his thoughts focused on his ex-wife, Helen, and her long, curly, soft red hair.

They met at a deposition because Helen was a witness to a bank robbery and Ray had subpoenaed her to the court reporter's office. She was the only eyewitness that had picked Ray's client out of a six-pack picture lineup. When she walked into the deposition room, Ray was smitten by her hourglass figure and shiny red hair. The prosecutor explained the deposition process to Helen and then the court reporter swore Helen to tell the truth.

During the deposition, Ray aggressively questioned her memory of the robber's clothes, facial hair, and physical characteristics. She was not shaken by Ray's detailed questions and answered him forcefully and unequivocally. At the end of the hour-long deposition Ray asked, "Is it possible that you might have picked the wrong man?"

Helen smiled and stared back at Ray for three seconds before answering. "Is it possible for you not to look at my ass as I walk out the door?"

Helen got up and walked out of the deposition room. The prosecutor looked at the court reporter and said in a superior tone, "Let the record reflect that Mr. Harrison did indeed stare at the witness's posterior as she walked out the door."

Needless to say, Ray's client was convicted at trial. Two months later at a charity formal for the American Heart Association, Ray saw Helen talking to an older man that looked vaguely familiar. Ray made his way across the room and caught Helen's eye as he approached. She smiled and tugged on the man's arm. "Look, Mr. Richmond, it's the defense lawyer from the trial."

The man turned and looked at Ray, "Good evening, counselor. Good to see you again."

Helen saw Ray's confused look, "Why, Mr. Harrison, don't you recognize the jury foreman, Louis Richmond?"

Ray apologized for his poor memory, and the three of them discussed the highlights of the trial. Helen was wearing a low-cut emerald evening gown with spaghetti straps that contrasted nicely with her red hair. Her long curly hair fell a few inches over her sun-freckled shoulders. Ray remembered very little of the conversation with Louis Richmond because he was staring at Helen the entire time, and she happily returned his lustful gaze. Ray may not have won the trial, but he won the key witness's heart. Three months later Ray proposed and they were married soon after, a June wedding at Helen's Baptist Church.

Ray and Helen honeymooned in Tahiti for a week. They swam and sunned at the beach all day and danced all night under the tropical moon before having passionate sex every night. It was just as Helen had dreamed her honeymoon would be, and they swore their undying love for each other.

Unfortunately, after the honeymoon they returned to reality. The wedding and honeymoon drained a large portion of Ray's savings, but he didn't care because he was in love. Helen was pregnant within six months with Beth, and Ray was thrilled. Helen seemed to enjoy being a stayat-home mom, and four years later she was pregnant with Julie. After Julie was born Helen never seemed the same. At first Ray just told himself that is was post-partum blues, but as Helen's complaints increased he started staying out late, drinking more, avoiding coming home to a guaranteed fight.

Of course, it only delayed and intensified the

preordained fight between them. Helen didn't care for her husband's new hobby and told him so every night. Neither one of them backed down and they stayed angry at each other. After six months of fighting, Helen filed for divorce, shortly after she started her affair with Larry Alston.

Chapter 4

Tuesday morning, 8:45 a.m.

The Lee County Courthouse and County Jail were in a seven story building, six stories open to the public and the top floor used for transporting prisoners and debriefing jail house snitches away from prying eyes and ears at the jail. It was painted a pale yellow and had minimal windows because the courthouse selection committee picked the lowest bid for construction. The courtrooms were on the fifth floor and labeled with letters from A to H. All of the courtrooms were finished in oak wood with carpeted floors that absorbed sound and magnified the bad acoustics of the ridged oak panels on the courtroom walls. Microphones and amplifiers were required to make the courtrooms functional.

Judge Stalman used courtroom H, and his office was directly below it on the fourth floor. He walked up a hidden stairwell to a secure hallway that lead to his courtroom. The hallway also had a conference room and bathroom on each side. The doorway at the end of the secure hall opened ten feet from Judge Stalman's bench. On the opposite side of the bench, another hallway lead back to the holding cell for in-custody defendants.

Ray walked behind the wall separating the courtroom from the hallway to the holding cell for the in-custody defendants, brought over from the county jail. The holding cell was a twelve foot by sixteen foot room separated from the main hall by a heavy metal door painted gray to help drown out the sounds of caged humans. The holding cell consisted of three cement walls painted pale yellow, and the entry area of gray metal bars from floor to ceiling, with a lockable swinging door. There was a stainless commode with no privacy panels and a small sink on the back wall. Stainless steel benches lined the side walls. The caged area started four feet back from the heavy metal door. This four-foot uncaged space was for the defense lawyer, where he could stand and talk to his client. The smell of panicked human sweat had fused with the paint and was always present. As more defendants become packed into the caged area, other unsavory odors increase. This was the stage where a defendant decided to accept a plea offer from the State or go to trial.

On this day, Dallas was the only defendant in the holding cell because his case was the only thing on the docket. At the beginning of the trial, Ray brought over enough clothes for him to have a different outfit each day. Dallas was changing from his red jailhouse jumpsuit into his street clothes as Ray walked through the heavy metal door. He looked up at Ray and asked, "Why do I have to wait and put my belt on when I go into the courtroom?"

Ray answered, "That's the protocol. In the past, some poor bastard became despondent and hanged himself with his belt while waiting for the trial to start."

Dallas rolled his eyes, "Oh, great. Thanks for the encouragement."

Ray shrugged his shoulders, "Hey, you asked."

Dallas took a deep breath, grabbed the metal bars with both hands, and looked nervously at Ray. "Well, what do you think?"

Ray leaned against the wall and answered, "I think we got a good jury. They were listening to me in opening statement. The paper and TV stations have been pretty fair in their reporting about this being a circumstantial case. I think the jury is looking forward to a good show."

Dallas squeezed the bars and raised his voice, "This isn't a fucking show! It's my life!"

Ray stared at Dallas and was quiet for a few seconds. He continued in a somber tone, "I know it's your life, Dallas.

I'm going to do everything in my power to get you acquitted. But make no mistake about it—the jury wants to be entertained. They've seen TV shows and movies and they want us to entertain them while I show the State doesn't have proof beyond a reasonable doubt. We have to make them think you are an innocent man."

Dallas pleaded, "But I am innocent."

Dallas walked over and slumped on to the stainless bench. Ray finally had him where he wanted him. "I know, but the jury has to be convinced. I don't want you rolling your eyes or pounding the table. Juries like polite defendants, so I'm going to give you a sheet of paper and pen. If you disagree with what a witness says, write it down. I can't listen to what a witness is saying and what you are saying at the same time."

Dallas nodded solemnly. Ray said, "The bailiffs will bring you out in just a second. And remember all your tricks from making real estate sales. We are trying to sell the jury on your innocence."

Both men were silent as they contemplated the trial. After a few seconds, Ray smiled and said, "Oh, and by the way, I think that one divorced female juror with the three kids was checking you out."

Dallas's eyes lit up and he smiled. "Really? I was trying to flirt with her a little bit."

Ray snickered, "A little bit goes a long way.

Remember, be polite, and don't act like you're in a singles' club."Dallas nodded.

As Ray walked out of the holding cell, Dallas was smiling. Ray didn't know if Dallas had made a connection with the juror or not, but he had to get Dallas out of his depressed mood. Dallas's ego was as big as his prostate.

As Ray walked back to the courtroom, he thought of how hard the past eight months had been on Dallas while he was held in the county jail with no bond. He was a very successful real estate developer, but all of his projects had been put on hold or fallen through since his arrest. He had fully mortgaged his properties to pay his legal bills and normal monthly obligations. Dallas was either going to prison for life or he was going to be acquitted. Ray was glad Dallas didn't have his belt.

Each courtroom had a head bailiff and two assistant bailiffs. Each bailiff had a radio and a panic button attached to their uniform, along with pepper spray and an asp. Experienced inmates knew to stay away from the expandable asp. It was made of heavy industrial steel and compacted to ten inches. In case of a rebellious inmate, the bailiff could pull the asp out of its holster and snap it toward the floor.

It would expand out to a little over two foot in length and weighed over three pounds. If an inmate was struck in the small of his back or behind a knee, he would fall to the ground and beg for forgiveness.

If a bailiff was in a struggle and couldn't operate his radio call button, he could hit the panic button attached to his belt to send out an emergency signal to all bailiffs in the courthouse. The emergency signal would tell every bailiff which courtroom had the emergency. All of the bailiffs operated with the knowledge of a formidable backup force.

Whenever a panic button was deployed, the bailiffs raced to the signaled courtroom to subdue the problem inmate or rebellious civil litigant.

Spere was sitting at counsel table with his paralegal going over which witnesses were waiting in the witness room and which ones would be arriving later. As the paralegal was pushing her chair back to go out of the courtroom and make some cell phone calls to missing witnesses, she stared at Spere's left eye. Spere noticed and quickly looked down at his notes, hoping she couldn't see through the makeup covering a bruise under his left eye.

Spere's wife, Ethel, slapped him the night before because he forgot to put the damp laundry into the dryer. He'd been sitting at the dining room table reviewing witness statements for the trial when she left for her yoga class. On the way out of the door, she asked him to put the clothes in the dryer when they were finished washing. She came back two hours later and walked into the utility room. She let out a scream and walked straight up to Spere.

"I work too. I'm tired of you not helping me with the housework."

Ethel slapped him with an open hand and said in a flat voice, "Don't make me mad."

Spere's face was flushed with embarrassment. He wanted to get up and leave the house, but instead he walked toward the utility room. He said nothing, but he put the clothes in the dryer and turned it on. Ethel walked to the bathroom for her hot bath without saying a word.

Spere sat back down at the dining room table and tried to concentrate on his case. His anger and embarrassment were too much, so he got up and walked to the back yard for a cigarette. He lit up and sat down at his rickety picnic table. He never thought he would be a battered spouse, but that was what he'd become in the last year. Spere heard the neighbor's dog barking and looked over their fence. The dog had his front paws up on an oak tree, barking at a treed squirrel. Spere knew how the squirrel felt.

He couldn't tell anyone or go to counseling, because Ethel was the director of the domestic violence unit at the courthouse. Her job was to supervise all of the employees that took complaints from battered spouses and helped them get restraining orders against the abusing spouse. He was six feet tall and weighed 225 pounds. No one would believe his skinny wife slapped him around.

Spere knew that Ethel would help him put on makeup in the morning to cover the bruising. She always did.

** ** ** ** **

Ethel lit three large green candles on the window sill above the tub. She inhaled the evergreen scent as she turned the water off and slid into the warm bubble bath. She positioned her bath pillow on the rear of the tub and leaned back, resting her head. She felt her ribs and smiled because she'd learned over time she was at her desired weight whenever she was able to count her ribs by touch. She relaxed knowing her husband had put the laundry in the dryer without a fight.

Ethel met her husband while she was getting her master's in sociology, and he was in law school at the University of Miami. After one year of dating, she'd proposed to Spere when she graduated and he was in his second year of law school. He agreed and they went shopping for a ring. She picked out a square cut, two carat diamond with a platinum setting. Spere cautiously mentioned that it was a lot of money for a student, but she insisted, so they financed it.

After he graduated, they moved back to her hometown of Ft. Myers. She started work as a social worker and he started as a prosecutor. After five years of dealing with troubled families, Ethel took a job at the courthouse as a domestic violence advisor. She had worked her way up to supervisor of the department.

The trouble began one weekend when she went to a training seminar in Miami with four of her female co-workers. The keynote speaker had a PhD in psychology and had written three books on domestic violence. Most of what she talked about, Ethel had heard many times before. However, at the end of her speech the keynote speaker spoke of a new
trend in her practice. She called it the preppie problem.

The preppie problem was a new type of domestic violence between well-educated couples with successful careers and no children. The keynote speaker cautioned this situation led to competition among the spouses and, sometimes, a question of control. It was usually the man that was the abuser, but sometimes, the woman would be equally aggressive. As always, the keynote speaker suggested counseling to deal with the problem.

Ethel and her four co-workers went to happy hour at the hotel bar after the speech. After three pitchers of margaritas, they were all lit up pretty good. The other four went out for dinner, but Ethel had a headache so she went back to her room and ordered room service. She called Spere, but there was no answer. She spent the rest of the night calling and worrying about where her husband was. She called the next morning and there was no answer. As she packed her bags the next morning, she thought of the keynote speaker's message about the preppie problem.

Was Spere trying to control her by not telling her where he was? Was he having an affair? Was he trying to control whether or not she could relax by not telling her where he was? She decided she was not going to be a victim of control. When she got home in the afternoon she was the angriest she'd ever been. She walked in and saw a note on the dining room table. She grabbed it and read:

Gone camping.
Love, Brian.

Ethel considered her husband's intentions. Had he gone camping with friends? Were there females with them? Or was he really with a secret girlfriend in her apartment? The more she thought about it, the angrier she got. She deduced that he wanted to be in control and make her wonder where he was. She decided she was not going to be a victim of her husband's control.

She opened a bottle of wine and poured a large glass. She turned on the TV and switched to a show on cheating husbands. She curled up on her couch and considered why her husband would cheat on her as she listened to the program. They'd been married ten years and she had to admit the sex had definitely slowed down in the past few years. She forced herself to go back over the past year and compute the number of times they had sex. It was only five or six times in the past year. She poured a second glass of wine and considered the sobering fact that they'd only had sex an average of once every two months for the past year.

Ethel remembered back to her bachelorette party. After a few shots of tequila, one of her friends asked her whether she liked her penises big or small. She smiled and announced to her friends that she didn't care whether they were big or small, but she liked them busy. Her friends all cheered and everybody had toasted to busy penises.

The first few years of marriage, Spere had been busy at home and at the office. It seemed the past few years he was just busy at the office. Ethel considered her husband's declining sex drive and realized it was related—he wanted to be in control of sex. He had intentionally slowed down having sex with her because he wanted to be in control. And maybe save it for his girlfriend?

As Ethel poured a third glass of wine, she swore to herself that she was not going to be a victim of her husband's control. She sat back down on the couch and considered her predicament. She was just finishing her wine, when Spere walked in the door and called across the room, "Hey honey, how are you doing?"

Ethel didn't say anything as she stood up and walked toward her smiling husband.

Spere opened his arms to hug her as he said, "Did you learn anything good at the seminar?"

Ethel thought she heard a mocking tone in her husband's voice. Spere leaned down to kiss Ethel and she slapped him hard with her open right hand.
Spere jumped back. "Ow! What the hell was that for?"

Ethel stepped forward and slapped him again. He backed up and sat down at the dining room table, shocked by her slaps. Ethel proceeded to chew him out for not calling her and accused him of cheating. Spere was mystified and his face hurt, so he just let her rant until she finally calmed down. He apologized for not calling and assured her there was no girlfriend. They kissed and the kiss became passionate with groping hands on both sides. They stumbled into the bedroom and had incredible makeup sex.

The next morning Ethel woke up with a smile. She

liked being in control and she liked her husband busy. For the past year, Ethel would pick a fight with her husband, slap him, apologize, and have makeup sex. She knew it was weird, but she liked it.

Chapter 5

Tuesday morning, 9:00 a.m.

Judge Stalman was a formidable figure. He was six-foottwo-inches and a fit 210 pounds. He played racquetball at the local health club during the week and golf on the weekends. His gray hair was receding, so he tried to make up for it by growing a beard. The beard apparently had a sense of humor and came in completely white. His barber trimmed his beard daily and cut his scalp hair every other week.

"All rise. The Honorable Gary Stalman is presiding over this court."

Judge Stalman walked up the steps to his bench and sat down. He swiveled in his chair and looked out at the litigants and the audience over his brown reading glasses. This was the part he liked most about being a judge. He could immediately tell everyone to sit down or he could hesitate and see how many people would sit down within a few seconds out of habit. He would turn and stare at the offending fastsitters until they stood back up out of embarrassment.

He decided to lull everybody into a quick seat pattern and then get a few of them after lunch. In a deep baritone he bellowed, "You may be seated."

After everyone sat down, Judge Stalman looked at Spere. "Call your first witness."

Spere stood and announced, "The State calls Armando Ruiz."

The bailiff walked to the witness room, opened the

door, and beckoned Mr. Ruiz into the courtroom. Mr. Ruiz emerged and slowly walked into the courtroom, packed with the media representatives, curious onlookers, and courthouse personnel. Mr. Ruiz was a middle-aged Hispanic of average build who had never been recognized as someone of importance. He did not relish walking into a brightly lit courtroom full of curious people.

The clerk spoke in a practiced voice. "Raise your right hand. Do you swear or affirm what you say will be the truth and nothing but the truth?"

Mr. Ruiz raised his left hand, looked at Judge Stalman, and announced, "Nothing but the truth. Or the truth. Whatever you want, Your Honor."

People in the courtroom quietly laughed and looked cautiously at Judge Stalman for his reaction. Judge Stalman sat up in his seat and realized the courtroom was waiting for his Solomon-like response to this simple-minded witness. He cleared his throat and smiled at Mr. Ruiz. "Please raise your other right hand, Mr. Ruiz."

Everyone laughed nervously, and Mr. Ruiz realized his mistake. He raised his right hand and apologized.

Judge Stalman boomed, "Mr. Ruiz, do you swear what you say is the truth?"

"I do, Your Honor."

Judge Stalman hesitated for a few seconds and made sure everyone in the courtroom was looking at him before he announced, "Mr. Spere, you may proceed."

"Mr. Ruiz, please tell the court what you do for a living."

"I clean up at the Edison home."

"Let me direct your attention back to January eighteenth of this year. Did you find anything unusual when you started work that morning?"

Mr. Ruiz nodded. "Well, I drove my golf cart around the grounds that morning emptying the trash cans. They were overflowing from the party the night before. When I went to the garage area, I saw the garage doors were closed."

"Was it unusual for the garage doors to be closed?"

"Yes, they're normally left open. I pulled open the left door and turned on the lights. And that's when I saw him."

"Saw who?"

"The dead man."

Spere hesitated to let it sink in. He raised his voice, "Tell the jury exactly where the dead man was."

Ruiz leaned forward and said respectfully, "He was in the driver's seat of the old car. His body was tied with a rope to the seat, and his hands were wrapped with a bungee cord to the steering wheel. His front was bloody, and he leaned to one side. There were a lot of flies buzzing around."

"Was he wearing any clothes?"

Ruiz shook his head and said quietly, "No, señor."

Spere shrugged his shoulders and raised his hands in a questioning manner as he asked, "What did you do next?"

Ruiz raised his right hand to his chest and crossed himself, "I asked St. Francis to help me. And then I called the police on my cell phone."

"No other questions, Your Honor."

Spere sat down, and Judge Stalman looked at Ray. "Mr. Harrison, your witness."

Ray stood up and walked toward the podium, "Good morning, Mr. Ruiz."

"Good morning, señor."

"Was anything out of place or taken from the garage?"

"No, I checked after the police moved the body." "Was

there a sign of a struggle around the old car?"

Mr. Ruiz cocked his head to one side and asked, "What do you mean by 'sign of struggle?'"

Ray rephrased his question. "Was anything in the garage knocked over or out of place?"
Mr. Ruiz shook his head. "No, señor." "No further questions, Your Honor."

Judge Stallman bellowed, "You are dismissed, Mr. Ruiz."

Ruiz got out of the chair and scampered out of the courtroom before anyone changed his mind. Judge Stalman looked over at Spere. "Call your next witness."

Spere looked over at his paralegal in the back of the courtroom and she nodded. Spere announced, "The State calls Officer Delbert."

The assistant bailiff opened the witness room and called his name. A blue uniformed officer walked from the witness room door, and the clerk swore him in. He quickly walked to the witness stand and sat down. He looked up and smiled at Spere.

Spere asked, "Please tell us your name and where you work."

"My name is Steve Delbert, and I work for the Ft. Myers Police Department."

"Did you respond to a 911 call from the Edison Home on the morning of January eighteenth of this year?"

"Yes, I did."

"Tell the jury what you found when you got there."

Officer Delbert shifted in his chair and looked directly at the jury. "When I walked up to the garage, I could see three maintenance workers gathered outside of the garage area.

They pointed toward the garage, which had a single
44

light on. I walked in the open garage doors and saw the body in an old black Ford. I shined my flashlight in the car, and I could see a bloody white male. He was nude and his body was tied with a blue rope to the seat. His hands were fastened to the steering wheel with a yellow bungee cord, and his head was slumped down to his right."

Spere hesitated to let the gory details sink in with the jury before he continued. "Officer, could you see what caused the bloody wounds?"

The officer turned back toward Spere and ran his right hand through his hair. "I got up close and shined the light at his torso. There appeared to be at least two bullet holes in the chest, through the heart."

Spere nodded. "What did you do then?"

"I called the duty detective and then the medical examiner on my cell. I grabbed some evidence tape from my trunk and wrapped it around the entire garage area."

Spere looked up at Judge Stalman, "No further questions."

Judge Stalman looked at Ray and nodded. "Cross?"

Ray approached the podium, "Officer, did you ever shine the flashlight on the victim's face."

"Yes, I did."

Ray raised his voice, "Isn't it true the victim had a smile on his face?"

Ray heard two of the jurors let out a quiet gasp. The officer shifted in his seat and seemed to be uncomfortable. He answered, "Well, yes. But I don't know what caused it or if the body somehow moved after he died, or something."

Ray picked up the officer's statement and held it up. "Officer, didn't you state in your report that the victim had a smile on his face?"

"Yes, I did."

"No other questions, Your Honor."

Judge Stalman looked at the witness. "You are excused, sir."

As the officer stepped down, Judge Stalman looked at Spere, "Next witness."

"The State calls Jonathon Augustine."

The assistant bailiff opened the witness room and called his name. A tall, lanky man walked from the witness room in a seersucker suit, white shirt, and yellow bowtie. His silver hair was slicked back and his tan, chiseled cheeks were freshly shaved. He was sworn in by the clerk and sat down in the witness stand.

"Please tell the jury your name and where you live." "My name is Jonathon Augustine the fourth, and I live on McGregor Boulevard, just a couple of hundred yards south of the Edison Home. When I walk to the end of my dock, I can see the back side of the Edison Home."

"Mr. Augustine, please tell us your connection to the Edison Historical Society."

"I am the current president of the Edison Historical Society, and I have been associated with the Edison Home all my life."

Spere motioned with his open right hand toward the jury. "Mr. Augustine, please tell the jury the history of the Edison Home and the Edison Historical Society."

Augustine sat back in his chair and thought of his self-serving story. After a few seconds, he spewed forth his practiced speech: "Well, as you know, Mr. Edison and his wife, Mina, made a winter home here in Ft. Myers in the early 1900s. Mr. Edison enjoyed his winters here in Ft. Myers and started a nursery of Central and South American plants that he tried to use for industrial purposes. He was a

46

very generous benefactor of our young city. My father was one of his earliest employees at the estate."

Spere asked, "Could you tell the jury how the Historical Society was formed?"

Augustine sat forward in his seat and leaned toward the microphone. "As you know, Mr. and Mrs. Edison paid for all the palm trees to be planted up and down McGregor Blvd.

After Mr. Edison died, Mrs. Edison spent her later years trying to make Ft. Myers a better place to live. She sponsored plays and children choirs around Christmas and the other holidays.

"In her will, she left the Edison Estate to the City of Ft. Myers for display to the public to honor her late husband. The concerned citizens of Ft. Myers formed our non-profit group, the Edison Historical Society, to benefit the preservation of Mr. and Mrs. Edison's heritage to the City of Ft. Myers."

Spere nodded. "Can you tell the jury how the Edison Historical Society has benefited the Edison Home?"

"We assisted the Edison Home, along with other groups, in refurbishing the estate to its original look. Our current mission is to assist the City of Ft. Myers in making the Edison Home an enjoyable place for tourists to visit." "Mr. Augustine, when you say assist the City of Ft. Myers with the Edison Home, do you mean financial assistance?"

Augustine snickered, "What other kind of assistance is there?"

Spere continued, "Tell the jury how much money the Edison Historical Society raises with its annual fundraiser?"

Augustine looked up to his left and did a quick

calculation. "The past few years, we have raised approximately $700,000 per year with the annual ball and all of our generous sponsors."

Spere slowly flipped over a few pages of his legal pad at the podium and asked, "Mr. Augustine, were you at the annual fundraiser on January seventeenth of this year?" Augustine nodded, "Yes, I was."

"Did you notice an argument between the defendant, Dallas Kelley, and the victim, Bryce Cervante?" Augustine raised his voice, "Yes, I did." "Could you tell the jury about it?"

Augustine shifted in his chair and looked at the jury. "Yes, I can. I'm at the bar ordering a martini when I hear Dallas yelling. He's screaming at Bryce about screwing him out of money. All of us look up and hope it's a bad joke. We quickly realize that it's no joke—Dallas is uncontrollably angry."

"Mr. Augustine, was this a normal type of argument? "Oh, no. I've never heard someone so mad; Dallas was turning red and screeching like a baby bird."

Ray stood up, "Objection, opinion testimony."

Judge Stalman hesitated and made sure every eye in the courtroom was looking at him before he said firmly, "Objection sustained."

Ray looked at his client and noticed his face was red and his fingers were moving up and down like he was playing chopsticks on the piano. Ray leaned forward in his chair, trying to shield his client from inquisitive looks from the jury. He leaned toward his client and whispered, "Settle down and take a deep breath. Pick up the pen and draw a picture of this guy getting eaten by a shark."

Dallas looked wide-eyed at Ray and whispered, "Eaten by a shark?"

48

Ray put his left hand on Dallas's back and whispered, "That's what's going to happen on cross-examination."

Dallas smiled as picked up his pen and started drawing a large shark eating a jackass.

Spere asked, "How did the disturbance at the bar end?"

Augustine sat back in his chair and smiled. "One of Ft. Myers' finest was working security detail that night. He heard the commotion and came over. He stood between them and told Dallas he was going to have to leave. He escorted Dallas to his car and, fortunately, the fundraiser continued without any other problems that night. My compliments go out to the police department."

"No other questions, Your Honor."

Judge Stalman looked over at Ray. "Cross-examination?"

Ray nodded and stood up. He walked toward the podium with a single piece of paper and an old black and white picture. He set the picture on the podium and looked at the witness. "Good morning Mr. Augustine."

"Good morning, counselor."

"Did the victim, Bryce Cervante, have a date that evening?"

"No, not that I remember."

"Oh, really? Did Mr. Cervante not like women?"

Augustine started chuckling. He cleared his throat after a few seconds and answered, "No, that's not true. He loved women; maybe too much."

"Is it fair to say that Mr. Cervante was a playboy?"

"That's a fair statement."

"Do you know how many women at the party he had dated in the past?"

"I have no idea."

Ray stared at the witness for a few seconds and waited

for the jury's full attention. "Isn't it true that it's sort of a tradition for people at the fundraiser to have sex in public places late at night after most people have left?"

There were murmurs in the audience area, and all of the jurors glared at Ray. Spere started to object, but noticed the angry jurors. He decided to let Ray hang himself.

Augustine boomed, "Of course not. That sort of thing never happens at the Edison Home."

Ray smiled and picked up the piece of paper and the old photograph. He looked at both of them and then back at Augustine. Everyone in the courtroom was staring at Ray. He waited a few more seconds and looked back at Augustine and asked, "Could you tell the jury who your date was to the annual fundraiser during your junior year of college?"

Spere sensed a problem for his witness and jumped up as he yelled, "Objection, relevance."

Judge Stalman looked over at Ray, "Counselor, where is this going?"
Ray answered, "May we approach, Your Honor?" Judge Stalman nodded and answered sternly, "Yes, please do."

Spere, Ray, and the court reporter huddled at the front of the bench. Ray strategically placed himself closest to the witness so he could hear the whispered argument and see Ray's exhibits.

Judge Stalman looked at Ray. "How is this relevant, Mr. Harrison?"

Ray held up the piece of paper and the picture. "Your honor, my investigator got a sworn statement from a Ms. Annette Smith about her date with Mr. Augustine during their junior year of college to the annual fundraiser. I also have a picture of them together in their formal wear that night to refresh Mr. Augustine's memory, if needed."

Ray held the picture at an angle so Augustine could see it from the witness stand and continued. "During the fundraiser, Mr. Augustine and Ms. Smith went to the second floor of the Edison Home, which is not open to the public, and had a sexual encounter. It seems Mr. Augustine had a pass key to the estate he got from his father.

"In addition, Your Honor, on that same night after he abandoned his date, Mr. Augustine had a sexual encounter with another woman in the museum of the Edison Home. He later admitted that to Ms. Smith and she became very angry, and broke off their relationship."

Ray paused to let it sink in. "So, Your Honor, this witness denied that it was a tradition to have sex in public places at the Edison Home, late at night, during the annual fundraiser. I want to be able to cross-examine him about events that contradict what he said on the witness stand under oath."

Judge Stalman scratched his chin. "Assuming you caught the witness in a lie, how is that relevant to this case?"

Ray continued, "Your Honor, the victim in this case was found nude in a public place, tied up without a sign of a struggle. It is a logical suggestion that he was engaged in some type of sexual escapade involving bondage in a public area. And let's not forget the smile on the victim's face. Your Honor, if that happened, then the victim was shot by his lover, or her angry husband, and the gun was planted in my client's car. Therefore, I think the jury should be allowed to hear about other unusual sexual escapades that occurred at prior fundraisers at the Edison Home. Especially when this witness has lied under oath about his knowledge of prior escapades."

Spere was fuming. "Judge, this is nothing but a smoke screen. Mr. Harrison is trying to divert attention from his client. It doesn't matter what Mr. Augustine did thirty years ago while he was in college."

Judge Stalman ran his right hand through his hair and scratched the back of his head. After a few seconds of considering the situation, Judge Stalman said, "If the witness had said he was aware of prior sexual escapades, I would not allow this line of questioning. However, by him denying the prior sexual escapades he has opened the door. I am going to allow Mr. Harrison to cross-examine the witness about this." Spere was shaking. "But Judge, this is highly improper."

Judge Stalman glared at Spere. "Counselor, I've made my ruling. Sit down."

They returned to their places in the courtroom. Ray leaned on the podium and stared at Augustine. Augustine's color had turned to a pale ash and beads of sweat were forming on his brow. Judge Stalman looked at Ray, "You may continue."

"Could you tell the jury who your date was to the annual fundraiser here at the Edison Home during your junior year of college?"

Augustine slumped in his chair and answered quietly, "Annie Smith."

"During your date, did you go upstairs at the Edison Home?"

"Yes, we did."

"Isn't the upstairs area closed to the public?"

"Yes, it is. But I had made a copy of my father's pass key."

There were a few gasps in the courtroom. Ray looked

to the back of the courtroom and saw his investigator, Doug Shearer, and Annette Smith sitting in the back row. Ms. Smith had a smile on her face.

"What happened when you went upstairs with Ms. Smith?"

Augustine shifted in his seat. "Well, we made out on an old couch."

"Does that mean you had sex with her?"

Augustine looked like he was trying to pass a kidney stone. He whispered, "Yes."

The courtroom was abuzz, and Judge Stalman banged his gavel while yelling, "Order in the court."

Ray waited a few seconds. "What did you do next?" "We went back downstairs and rejoined the party." "Isn't it true, you left Ms. Smith and went down to the river with a couple of your friends and a whiskey bottle?"

"Yes."

"Isn't it true, Ms. Smith was angry that you left her and she got a ride home?"

"Yes."

"After you and your friends finished the whiskey bottle, you returned to the party, didn't you?" "Yes."

"Mr. Augustine, did you start talking to another girl when you returned to the party?"

Augustine turned to the judge and pleaded. "Do I have to answer these questions?"

Judge Stalman loved it and he glared at the beaten man. "Yes, you do."

Ray repeated, "Mr. Augustine, did you start talking to another girl when you returned to the party?"

"Yes."

"Isn't it true, she was drunk?"

"Yes."

"Isn't it true, you used your pass key to take her to the museum area of the Edison Home?"

"Yes."

"Isn't it true, you had sex with this second girl on the carpet next to the historic phonographs?"

There were gasps in the courtroom, and Judge Stalman banged his gavel. "Quiet in the courtroom."

Judge Stalman glared at Augustine. "Answer the question."

Augustine let out a loud breath and his voice cracked as he answered, "Yes."

There was silence in the courtroom as Ray walked back toward his table. He stopped half way there and looked back at Augustine. "Oh, I have one more question. Isn't it true, the second lady was Annette Smith's younger sister?" Augustine looked down and whispered, "Yes." "No other questions."

Judge Stalman looked at Spere. "Any redirect?" Spere answered quietly,

"No."

Judge Stalman looked at the jury, "We're going to break for lunch. I'll see you back here at one o'clock."

Chapter 6

Tuesday noon

The waitress at the Veranda approached the table and asked Ray and Doug for their order. They both ordered the fried green tomato salad and iced tea. It was an overcast day and the temperature was about ten degrees cooler than normal, so they were sitting on the brick patio, underneath an umbrella.

Ray asked, "How did Ms. Smith handle her family's dirty laundry getting aired out thirty years later?"

Doug laughed before answering. "She loved it. Back then, the sisters got in a big catfight, and the younger sister went to live with her aunt up in Tampa for a few years. That guy was such an asshole; he bragged to all his friends about it afterwards. That's how I found out about it. I hit all the bars the old timers frequent and asked about dirt on the guy. One of his old cronies told me the story and I tracked down Ms. Smith. She was reluctant at first to confirm it in writing. But I convinced her it was essential to question his credibility in front of the jury."

Doug waived to a friend on the other side of the restaurant and continued, "While I was waiting for you in front of the courthouse, Augustine and his wife walked by. She was chewin' him a new one."

They both laughed as the waitress brought them their iced tea. Ray took a swallow and looked around the table to make sure no one from the courthouse was nearby.

Ray asked, "You got anything new for me?"

Doug leaned forward and lowered his voice. "Well,

this morning at the Farmer's Market, I was eating breakfast with a few of my old buddies from the police department. They were talking about all of the kinky shit on the victim's computer at his house."

Ray cocked his head. "What kind of kinky shit?"

"A bunch of videos of young oriental women wearing black leather, spanking naked old white guys with whips. After they spanked the shit out of these old farts, they'd tie 'em up spread eagle on the bed with ropes. They'd get feathers and tickle these old guys 'til they pissed themselves." Ray leaned back in his chair and whistled.

"Weird shit.

Anything else from the computer?"

"A few pictures of topless celebrities."

The State Attorney's Office had failed to disclose this to him with all of the discovery material for trial. Ray wondered if the cops had even given it to Spere. If Spere had been given the information and failed to disclose it to the defense, he was in violation of ethics rules. Ray was thinking of how to use this new information at trial as the waitress brought them their salads. They talked about how the trial was progressing as they ate their lunch.

Doug had worked at the Lee County Sheriff's Office for seventeen years. He started as a road deputy after college and rapidly rose through the ranks. After five years on road duty he got promoted to detective. He loved solving crimes and tracking down the bad guys, at least until he became a suspect in his fiancée's murder and saw law enforcement in a different light. He was exonerated when he tracked down the murderer and killed him in a bloody fight on a stolen yacht.

Doug's view of the sheriff department changed and he had very strong feelings against a few of his superiors, who
56

once thought he was capable of killing his fiancée. Doug retired from the sheriff's office and opened up his own business as an investigator. His business flourished because all of the lawyers that had worked with him knew his talents. Half of his business was tracking down cheating spouses and the other half was assisting criminal defense lawyers investigating crimes their clients were accused of committing. Needless to say, Doug left no stone unturned.

Ray had first met Doug when he'd been court-appointed to defend a drifter, Amos Compton, accused of murdering another homeless man because he wanted his sleeping bag on a cold night. There were three homeless people that had supposedly seen the dispute in a homeless camp in the woods at the edge of town. They claimed Amos had cut the victim's throat and taken the sleeping bag.

Doug had been the detective assigned the case and interviewed the three witnesses, who said they saw Amos slice the victim. Amos had refused to make a statement to Doug, who arrested him afterwards. After Ray had been appointed to represent Amos, he went and met with him at the jail.

Amos was cordial to Ray and denied committing the crime, but refused to talk about the facts of the murder. A month later, in the third meeting with Amos, he finally told Ray what had happened.

Amos had been diagnosed with terminal cancer in Chicago, but no one would give him any medication to ease the pain because he had no insurance. The Chicago winter became unbearable, so Amos hitched his way to Ft. Myers. The three witnesses and the victim had befriended him when he arrived at the homeless camp. He self-medicated with cheap wine and any other alcohol available.

One night the victim died in his sleep from alcohol poisoning. The three witnesses and Amos came up with the plan that Amos would cut his throat and let some of the blood spill out of the body. The three witnesses would walk to a convenience store and call the police, claiming they witnessed a murder. Amos would be arrested and receive medical treatment for his terminal cancer at the jail. Amos said it was easier to die in jail than on the streets.

Ray doubted Amos's story, so he checked with the jail infirmary regarding any treatment of Amos. To Ray's amazement, they told him they were giving him medication to ease the pain of the cancer. Amos was dead within three months.

After Amos's death, Ray called up Doug and told him the story. Doug tried to find the homeless witnesses to confirm the story, but they had amazingly left town. Doug double checked witness's stories a lot more thoroughly after that bizarre case.

Doug and Ray next crossed paths in a robbery case.

Doug had interviewed a lot of witnesses and came up with a suspect. He'd put together a six-pack lineup to show the victim of the robbery. The victim had picked Ray's client out of the lineup, and he was arrested. At trial, Ray aggressively cross-examined Doug about suggesting his client's picture to the victim. Doug held his ground, and the defendant was convicted as charged.

After Doug retired, he called Ray for private investigative work after being turned down by other lawyers. Ray remembered how thorough Doug had been in tracking down the robber and hired Doug immediately to work on two of his cases. Ray was Doug's first client and he never forgot it. He always made time to take Ray's calls no matter how busy he was.

After they finished lunch, Doug left to go work on another case, and Ray called his secretary to check on his other clients. After Ray finished talking to his secretary, he called his ex-wife.

Helen read her caller ID and answered on the third ring. "Hello Ray, how's the trial going?"

Ray's blood always pumped faster when he heard her voice. "As good as can be expected. We should finish in time for me to take the girls to dinner though."

"Come by the house when you finish. The girls were so excited to see their daddy on the news last night." Ray beamed. "Well good, I hope I don't disappoint them. I've got to get back to court; see you later." "Bye."

Chapter 7

Tuesday 1:05 p.m.

The head bailiff announced, "All rise. The Honorable Gary Stalman is presiding over this court."

Judge Stalman walked in and sat down. He looked around the room until he saw a man in the audience area slowly bending to sit down. He focused on the man for a few seconds until he looked up and saw Judge Stalman staring him down. He quickly straightened up.

The judge boomed, "Everyone may be seated. Mr. Spere, your next witness."

Spere announced, "The State calls Amy Shafer."

The assistant bailiff opened the witness room and called her name. A tall brunette with a shoulder length hair walked in from the witness room wearing khaki pants and a white cotton T-shirt with *Crime Scene Tech* printed on the back of the shirt in blue letters.

The clerk swore her in, and she stepped on the witness stand. She got situated in the chair and lifted the microphone to her level.

"Please give us your name and place of employment." "My name is Amy Shafer, and I work for the Ft. Myers Police Department as a crime scene technician."

"Did you work a crime scene at the Edison Home on the morning of January eighteenth of this year?"

"Yes, I did."

"Tell the jury what you saw when you arrived."

Ms. Shafer cleared her throat. "I parked in the lot and walked across McGregor Boulevard to the garage area. The area was surrounded by yellow evidence tape, and it was secured by an officer. He was responsible for keeping a log of who went in and out of the crime scene."

Spere nodded. "Was anyone inside this taped area when you arrived?"

"No."

"What did you do next?"

"The first thing I did was take photographs of the area." Spere looked at Judge Stalman. "Your Honor, may I approach the witness?"

Judge Stalman nodded.

"Yes."

Spere picked up a handful of 8"x10" photographs and approached the witness. He handed the pictures to the witness as he said, "I'm showing you State's Exhibits one through fifteen. Can you identify them?"

The witness methodically looked at every photograph. Judge Stalman moved forward in his chair and looked over the witness's shoulder at the photographs. When she finished she looked up and announced, "They are the pictures I took of the garage area that day."

Spere looked at the judge. "Your Honor, I move to introduce State's exhibits one through fifteen into evidence and publish them to the jury."

Judge Stalman looked over at Ray quizzically and asked, "Any objections?"

Ray stood up and proudly announced, "No objection." Judge Stalman looked over at Spere, "They are admitted. You may publish."

The head bailiff walked over to the witness and retrieved the photographs. He walked over to the jury and handed them to the nearest juror. She looked at the first one and passed it to the juror next to her. It took five minutes for the jury to look at all of the photographs. The head bailiff gathered all of the photographs and took them to the clerk, who filed them away.

Judge Stalman nodded to Spere, "Please continue." Spere asked, "What did you do next?"

"I put on my gloves and gathered two shell casings from the floorboard of the Model T. I marked them in an evidence bag and sealed them."

"Did you collect any other evidence?"

"I cut the bloody fabric from the driver's seat and retrieved two .22 caliber bullets from the foam in the seat. I marked them in an evidence bag and sealed them." "Did you find any other physical evidence?"

"No, I did not."

"Did your assistant dust for fingerprints while you collected this evidence?"

"Yes, but there were no usable prints found."

"Did the casings get dusted for prints?"

"Yes, but no prints were recovered."

Spere looked at his notes. "When you finished processing the crime scene, did you call your shift commander?"

"Yes."

"Did he tell you a potential murder weapon had been found in the defendant's car at the defendant's house?"

"Yes, he asked me to go to the defendant's house to retrieve the firearm."

"What did you see when you got to the residence?" "Two officers had wrapped crime scene tape around the entire property. One officer was at the front of the property with a log sheet and the other was at the rear of the property to protect the crime scene. No one got into the crime scene without checking in with either officer"

Spere nodded and hesitated before asking, "Did you retrieve the firearm from the defendant's car?"

"Yes, it was under the driver's seat. I bagged it and marked it."

"Did you look for any physical evidence in the defendant's house?"

"We did, but we didn't find anything else.

"What did you do with the evidence you collected?" "I sent the evidence to FDLE.

"Could you tell the jury what FDLE is?"

"That stands for Florida Department of Law Enforcement. They perform all the scientific tests and ballistic tests on evidence. They have modern labs and better equipment than our office."

"No other questions."

Judge Stalman looked over at Ray. "Cross-examination?"

Ray stood up. "Yes, Your Honor."

As Ray walked to the podium for his questioning, he couldn't believe that Spere hadn't shown the jury that his client's fingerprints weren't on the gun. He was excited about the prosecutor's mistake because he was going to be able to make points with the jury. Ray took a deep breath and asked, "Isn't it true, my client's fingerprints were not on the gun you collected from his car?"

Ms. Shafer nodded. "That's true. He must've used gloves."

Ray bit his tongue and silently cursed Spere for coaching his witness. He looked over at Spere and saw a slight smile. Ray looked up at the judge. "Objection, non-responsive to my question."

Judge Stalman ruled. "Sustained."

Ray looked back at the witness with her smug look. He
64

asked, "Isn't it true there were no gloves found at my client's house?"

"Yes, that's true. He must've thrown them out of his car after he drove back from killing the victim."
Ray was livid. "Objection, non-responsive."

Judge Stalman leaned forward and blared out, "Sustained. The witness will refrain from making gratuitous comments. Only answer the question that is posed to you," Judge Stalman glared as he asked, "Do I make myself clear?"

Ms. Shafer answered meekly, "Yes."

Ray looked over at Spere's smiling face and slowly shook his head. Spere had prepped the witness to make the damaging answers to his seemingly safe questions. Spere had set him up, and Ray had foolishly taken the bait. Ray looked back at the judge and said meekly, "No further questions."

As the witness stepped down, Judge Stalman looked at Spere. "Call your next witness."
Spere said, "Michael Jamison."

The assistant bailiff opened the witness room and called his name. A uniformed officer walked into the courtroom and was sworn by the clerk. After he sat down in the witness stand Spere asked, "Could you tell the jury your name and who you work for?"

"My name is Michael Jamison, and I work for the Ft. Myers Police Department."

"Officer, tell the jury what your involvement was in this case."

"I worked a security detail the night of the big party at the Edison Home. I had to escort the defendant away from the party because he got in a yelling match with the victim. I escorted him to his BMW, and as he was driving away he was yelling, 'Tell that cocksucker I'm not done with him.'"

"Did you think that was a threat?"

Ray started to object but he knew he'd lose, so he said nothing.

The officer nodded, "Yes, I thought it was a threat."

"How late did you work at the party that night?"

"I stayed until about one in the morning. Everybody had left except the cleaning crew."

"When did you go to work the next morning?"

"I got to work at nine, and that's when I heard about the murder."

"What did you do?"

"I told my supervisor about the night before. He called in the detective working the case, and we prepared an affidavit and request for a search warrant. We took it over to the courthouse to the duty judge, and she signed the search warrant. We drove to the defendant's house and told him about the search warrant."

Spere pointed to Dallas. "How did the defendant act?"

"He was mad. He said it was bullshit because he'd done nothing wrong. When we found the gun, he starts yelling that it's not his gun. He yelled even louder when we put the cuffs on him."

Dallas squirmed and started pounding his fingers on the table. Ray leaned over and whispered, "Settle down."

Dallas nodded and put his hands underneath his thighs. Spere said, "No further questions."

Judge Stalman looked over at Ray. "Cross?"

Ray stood up and walked to the podium as he asked,

"Officer, did my client resist you searching his house or his car?"

"Not really, he just ran his mouth."

"Did he act surprised when you found a gun in his

car?" "He acted surprised, but a lot of defendants act surprised when we catch them."

"Objection, non-responsive."

Judge Stalman smiled. "Overruled. You asked the question."

Ray looked over at Spere smiling smugly at the prosecution's table. He was tired of the dirty pool—it was time for payback. Ray looked at the witness. "Did you meet with the prosecutor to discuss your testimony for this case?"

"Uh, we met this morning before court."

"Did he tell you what questions to expect from me?"

"Uh, well, he said that you might ask some type of questions."

"Did he suggest how to answer my questions?"

Spere sprang to his feet, "Objection, my witness is not on trial."

Judge Stalman boomed, "Overruled. I'm just as curious as the jury about the answer."

Spere slumped into his seat and suddenly became absorbed with his notes. Ray looked back at the witness and pointed to Spere. "Did this prosecutor suggest how to answer my questions?"

The officer shifted in his seat and said, "We talked about how to answer questions if you tried to be sneaky."

Ray looked over at the jury and slowly shook his head. "No further questions."

As Ray walked back to counsel table, Dallas nodded and looked at the jurors. All of the jurors looked at Spere as Judge Stalman announced, "Next witness."

The next three witnesses related in excruciating detail the meticulous search of the defendant's vehicle and his home for some connection to the crime scene or the murder weapon. There was no evidence found, but Spere knew that if these witnesses weren't called, Ray would argue it was an incomplete investigation. They were boring witnesses who went on for hours, and some of the jurors were close to nodding off for an afternoon nap. After the last witness, Judge Stalman adjourned court until nine the next morning.

** ** ** **

Spere was raised on a farm in Eastman, Georgia until he was twelve. His parents divorced, and his mom moved to Tampa and married a criminal defense lawyer. Spere would listen to the stories his step-father told about getting guilty people off based on technicalities. Spere learned to hate the stories and the life of luxury his step-father lived. Late at night Spere would fantasize about being home on his father's farm in Georgia.

Spere majored in history at the University of Tampa and went to law school in Miami. He'd been a prosecutor for twenty years and loved it. He'd prosecuted all of the high profile cases for the past five years and only lost once. The only lost case was to Ray, so Spere was determined to get a guilty verdict to soothe his bruised ego.

Ray's client was a tenth grade teacher charged with having sex with one of her male students and master-minding her husband's murder for insurance money. The student had killed the teacher's husband and gotten caught. He immediately blamed his teacher and claimed she was the brains behind the crime. He pled to a reduced charge of manslaughter with ten years prison and agreed to testify against Ray's client, the schoolteacher. Ray destroyed the student's credibility on cross-examination with his inconsistent statements to police. The wife admitted the
68

affair, but claimed she never told him to kill her husband.

Ray got a not guilty verdict for the wife, and she collected a cool one million dollars from his life insurance company. The grieving widow quickly calmed her pain by spending it all within two months. Within a year she was in bankruptcy court over failed investments and a foreclosed home.

Spere never allowed himself to forget that loss to Ray.

Chapter 8

Tuesday evening, 6:08 p.m.

Ray slowed his black Lexus coupe as he approached the guard house at Paradise Preserve. Ray rolled down his driver's side window and waived to the security guard. "Here to pick up the kids, Rusty."

The gray-haired guard waved back as he opened the gate and quipped, "Have a nice night, Mr. Harrison."

Ray accelerated and drove around the serpentine road to Larry and Helen's house on the sixteenth green. Ray always had mixed feelings going to his ex-wife's new house. He loved seeing his girls, but to get them he had to see Helen, whom he still loved. As he turned into the cobblestone driveway, he saw Helen and the girls unloading her red Suburban.

Ray parked and stepped out of his car as his girls ran to him. Beth, fourteen, and Julie, ten, were very different creatures. Beth took after her mom—an out-going girl with growing curves and fiery red hair who loved boys. Julie was the quiet one who liked the internet and crossword puzzles. She was a tall, lanky brunette who had the same fair skin as Ray.

They ran up and both hugged Ray tightly. Julie said, "Dad, guess what? I googled you last night and you came up on twelve sites. That's so cool!"

Beth asked, "Are you still dating that blonde reporter? I love her new hair style."

Ray blushed when he looked up at Helen and she raised her left eyebrow and smiled mischievously. Ray sidestepped the question, "Daddy's been too busy with this trial to worry about anything else."

Julie asked, "Can we go to the Farmer's Market? I love their cornbread."

Ray answered, "Sure. Are you ready?"

Beth said, "In just a second. We're helping mom unload a new antique."

Ray looked over at the open rear cargo door and saw the Suburban was loaded down with a wooden chest. He said, "No problem, let me help."

As they walked over, Helen asked, "How's the trial going?"

Ray answered, "So far, so good. No physical evidence tying Dallas to the victim, except the gun."

Helen said, "That's a big deal, right?"

Ray answered, "The prosecutor thinks so."

Helen looked at the girls. "Go clean out a spot in the garage next to the jet skis so we can set this down. I need to clean it up."

The girls walked over to the garage and started stacking junk in a new pile. Ray walked over to the rear of the Suburban and asked, "What is it?"

Helen walked closer and pointed to the back of the chest, "It's a Florida Pine wardrobe chest from the mid 1800s. You can tell because of the wood pegs connecting the sections and the type of stain used. I'm gonna put it in the guest bedroom."

Ray stepped forward and grabbed the right side as he said, "Slide it back and we'll slowly lower it down."

Helen put up her hand, signaling Ray to stop. "Let me grab a couple of towels to put over the hitch and trunk clasp."

Helen reached into a plastic storage crate in the cargo

area and pulled out two towels. She laid them out over the metal protrusions and then nodded toward Ray. They slowly slid the chest out of the cargo area and set it on the driveway. Helen walked next to Ray and touched his back lightly. "Thanks for the help."

Ray could smell Helen's jasmine perfume. She'd worn the same brand since he'd met her and it drove Ray crazy. He'd smelled it on other women, but it was never the same. Something about Helen's body chemistry and the perfume allowed them to fuse together in a perfect tandem. Ray remembered how their bodies used to melt together after hours of making love. It had been a long time since Ray had been close enough to smell it. Their eyes met and Ray smiled. Helen looked away, and walked quickly toward the girls.

Helen said cheerfully to their daughters, "That looks good. Come on over here and we'll all move it into the garage."

Ray motioned and said, "Beth, come on my side. We'll all lift a corner and walk it over."

The former family moved the heavy antique into the garage without a scratch. Ray was still savoring Helen's perfume when Julie said, "Let's go eat. I'm hungry."

Ray said, "Last one to the car has to eat broccoli."

The girls squealed and raced to the Lexus. Ray looked wistfully at Helen, and she stepped forward and hugged Ray. Ray squeezed her as she said, "Thanks for the help."

Ray's senses were overwhelmed with Helen's touch and her overpowering scent. He pulled her closer and whispered, "It was good to see you."

Helen broke off the hug and stepped back. She knew Ray still cared for her, but the feeling was not mutual. She respected Ray for his responsible child support and the time he spent with the girls, but the fire was gone. As she quickly walked back to the Suburban to close the cargo door she said, "Have a good dinner."

Ray hesitated and took a deep breath. He looked back at his girls and smiled. They made goofy faces at him and giggled. As he walked toward his car he said, "I'll have them home by nine."

Helen answered politely, "No problem."

As Ray opened his door he heard Beth say from the passenger seat, "Oh shit. I forgot my ho-on-the-go bag." Ray looked at her incredulously. "What did you say?"

Beth opened her door as she said, "Oh, Dad. That's what all the girls call their backpacks."

Beth ran back to the Suburban and opened the rear passenger door. She grabbed her pink ho-on-the-go bag and ran back to the Lexus. Ray looked over to Helen, "Did you hear what she said?"

Helen laughed. "Get over it, Ray."

Ray was miffed but didn't want to create a scene. He got in his Lexus and looked in his rear mirror at Julie. She slowly shook her head in a disapproving manner as Beth switched the radio to a hip-hop station. Beth opened up her ho-on-the-go bag and showed Ray her latest photos. Ray had given both girls digital cameras for Christmas. Julie used hers for special occasions, but Beth used hers every day.

Ray drove toward the Farmer's Market as his girls told him about their latest adventures at school. The thirty minute ride passed quickly, and they pulled into the parking lot at seven.

The Farmer's Market was in the commercial area of the city. All of the local farmers used to bring their harvest to town and store it in warehouses until a tractor trailer or rail

74

car loaded it up. An enterprising family started a restaurant next to these warehouses for all of the hungry farmers and truckers. However, the excellent home-cooked food soon attracted many others. The farmers' warehouses closed over time, but the Farmer's Market restaurant was still the best place in town for southern cooking.

The restaurant itself was a plain cement block building painted baby blue, and the roof was tin. The interior walls and ceiling were painted white and the floor was painted red. The hungry customers sat at Quaker style tables and chairs. Next to the cash register was a display case with local honey and the latest gospel music for sale, reminding the visitor of the restaurant's proud southern roots.

The waitress grabbed the pencil from behind her ear as she asked, "What'll ya'll have?"

Beth said, "Meatloaf with mash potatoes."

Julie followed, "The vegetable plate with fried okra, buttered carrots, green beans and lima beans."

Ray smiled. "Fried chicken with macaroni and cheese, and tea for everybody."

The waitress nodded. "Rolls or cornbread." "Cornbread!" The girls said in unison.

The girls giggled, and the waitress smiled at Ray. Ray looked at Julie and remembered when he taught her how to play hide-and-seek when she was five. He had explained the rules to her and had told her he was closing his eyes and counting to twenty-five while she went and hid. After Ray had finished counting, he opened his eyes and saw Julie sitting in the same chair with her hands over her eyes.

Ray had asked, "Why didn't you hide?"

Julie had kept her hands over her eyes and had answered, "I did hide. You can't see me."

Ray had been confused. He had hesitated and said,

"You're right in front of me. Of course I can see you."

Julie had shaken her head and had whispered, "I can't see you, so you can't see me."

The waitress brought everyone their iced teas and brought Ray back from his day dream. Ray used Sweet'n Low for his tea, Beth used sugar, and Julie only squeezed a lemon. As the girls discussed the latest movies, Ray thought of each girl's hobbies. Beth liked hip-hop music and boys. She had an I-Pod with all of the latest music. Her cell phone ring was changed weekly based on the latest download, and her CD collection took up one wall of her bedroom. He tried to avoid thinking about her collection of boys.

Fortunately, Julie only liked soccer and crossword puzzles.

Ray was brought back to his daughters' conversation when the volume got louder. Julie blurted out, "Stop making fun of soccer."

Beth quipped, "Stop being a teacup."

Ray asked, "What's a teacup?"

Beth said, "Mom says women are either teacups or mugs. Mugs are strong, and it doesn't matter how hot the coffee is or where you put them in the dishwasher because they don't crack. Teacups are sensitive and can be cracked if you grab them too hard or put boiling water in them. Mom tells us we need to be mugs."

Fortunately, the waitress brought the food and everyone forgot the soccer dispute. As they were eating, Ray realized Beth was looking and sounding more like her mother every day. She had the red, curly hair and the quick wit. It was also painfully obvious to Ray that Beth's womanly curves were expanding noticeably.

When Ray had met Helen at twenty-one she was a 42C.

76

After having the two girls, her breasts had grown to 44DD, and Helen was not happy with their looks. Ray had told her she looked great, but Helen decided to have breast reduction surgery. The doctor reduced them to 42B, but Helen was only happy with them for seven months. She went back to the same doctor and had them enhanced to 42D. Within six months of the surgery, Helen had begun her affair with Larry Alston. She divorced Ray, and Larry married her ten months after the divorce was final.

After they finished dinner, Ray took the girls to Target for some shopping. Beth bought a new miniskirt and a CD while Julie bought a paperback novel and some plastic boxes for storing things. As they drove back to Helen's home, the girls talked about who was the cutest guy on TV. Beth liked Wilmer Valderama and Julie voted for George Clooney.

Ray pulled into Helen's drive and got out of his Lexus for goodbye hugs. He pulled both of them close and squeezed. After a few seconds, Julie stepped back and stuck out her right fist with her pinky extended. She smiled and said, "Dad, you promised to take us to the movies this weekend. Give me a pinky promise."

Beth held out her left fist with her pinky extended and said, "Come on, Dad."

Ray laughed and put out both of his fists with his pinky fingers extended toward his daughters' pinkies. His pinky fingers wrapped around theirs and he said, "I promise."

They smiled and hugged him again before they turned and walked to the front door. He watched them go inside, and he got back in his car and drove away. Ray remembered when they were little girls and shared a bedroom with matching single beds. He told them a bedtime story and tucked them in every night. Once Beth asked Ray to scratch an itch on her back, which he did. When he finished on the first spot, he moved down her back and hit a ticklish spot. Beth started squealing with delight and said "Stop tickling me."

Julie didn't want to be left out of the fun, so she said, "Dad, come ickle me."

Ray moved over to Julie's bed and said, "What's an ickle?"

Julie smiled. "It's part itch and part tickle."

Ray scratched Julie's back lightly until he hit a tender spot and she giggled.

Beth squealed, "Dad, come ickle me."

As Ray drove home, he wiped away the tears and felt an overwhelming desire for a drink. After he got home, he poured himself a scotch on the rocks and turned his stereo to the classical music station as Caesar jumped on his leg, wanting more attention. He sat his drink on the dining room table, walked into the kitchen, and opened up his storagedrawer, overflowing with pictures and letters from his daughters. He pulled out the most recent letters from each and walked back to his lonely drink at the dining room table. He sat down and read Beth's most recent letter:

Dear Dad,

Thanks for letting me spend Saturday night with my girlfriends.

We went to the movies and then got pizza. My old boyfriend was there and got mad when I ignored him. Whatever!

Cheerleading practice starts next week. Mom is the coolest of all the moms. She takes us to R movies and lets us surf the internet. Oops, I guess I'm not

supposed to tell you.
Love, Beth

Ray felt his temper flaring up, but he took a good pull and reached down to pet Caesar. Caesar leaned into Ray's leg and enjoyed the scratch behind the ears. After another pull, he calmed down and read Julie's most recent letter:

Dear Daddy,
I miss you. I know you've very busy, but I wanted you to know that I think about you a lot. I wrote a poem just for you.

The Lizard

Every morning I open my bedroom blind. A green lizard is always outside on the sill. He looks so gentle and kind. I imagine he stays there all night until he sees me awake and fine.

Daddy, you are like the lizard. You always look out for me even if you're not always inside the house with us. Love, Julie

Caesar yelped so Ray let him outside to do his business in the fenced in back yard. Ray drained his glass and wiped away a tear.

Chapter 9

Tuesday evening, 9:23 p.m.

Ray heard Caesar barking from the back yard. Ray let him in, and Caesar jumped up on Ray's leg. He scooped him up and carried him into the kitchen while petting him behind the ears. He let him down and refilled his drink. Caesar started barking over some sound in the back yard. After a long pull, he walked over to the back door and let Caesar back out.

Ray paid one of his retired neighbors to come by in the middle of the day and let Caesar out. But on days he worked late, or when he had dinner with the girls, Ray always felt guilty about leaving Caesar home alone. Caesar was always good about holding it in until Ray got home, but he still felt guilty.

Ray had gotten Caesar after his divorce and felt a special friendship with him. After all, Caesar had listened to him rant about the unfairness of the divorce after Ray drank too many scotches. Caesar never had too much to say, but he was a great listener. For the first year after the divorce, Ray didn't date. It was just Ray, Caesar, and cases of scotch.

Ray let Caesar in and filled up his food and water bowl. He turned his stereo to his favorite oldies station to change his mood. He sat down at the dining room table with his glass of scotch, a legal pad, and black, blue, and red pens. He listed all of the witnesses that would testify in black on the left hand column. After each witness, he wrote in red all of the facts that hurt his case, and in blue, all the facts that helped him. By the time he finished his list, his glass was empty. He walked into the kitchen and made another glass to help him concentrate.

As he sat down to compare all of the witnesses, Aretha Franklin's hit "A Natural Woman" came on the radio. He dropped his pen and took a gulp of his scotch. It was Helen's favorite song, and a flood of memories came crashing through his analytical process.

Helen's curly red hair hung six inches past her shoulders. It was very thick hair that she conditioned every day, and it was as soft as velvet. Every night she brushed it 100 times and Ray enjoyed watching because he knew what came next. Helen's favorite form of foreplay involved her hair. They would climb into bed nude and Ray would lay on his back with his arms and legs spread out. Helen wouldn't let him touch her until she'd given him a hair bath. A hair bath consisted of her crawling on all fours next to Ray and lowering her head close enough to his body so her hair would touch him. She would start at his head and slowly go down his body, pulling her hair back and forth. It took at least ten minutes before she made it to his toes.

It drove both of them absolutely crazy—at least for the first six years of their marriage. After that, Helen decided she didn't like hair baths anymore. Ray missed them, but he didn't complain because he was trying to keep her happy. He thought maybe the stress of the two girls was affecting her libido. Ray was working a lot and Helen was a stay-at-home mom.

One night Ray came home after a big trial, and there was a baby sitter watching the girls. He asked the sitter where Helen was, and she said she didn't know but that Helen asked her to stay until he came home. Ray paid the sitter and tried unsuccessfully calling Helen on her mobile.

Ray fell asleep in the family room watching TV until Helen came home at three in the morning and Ray woke up.

Ray asked angrily, "Where have you been?"

Helen slurred her words, "I've been out, Ray. I needed some time by myself."

Ray was hurt and angry, but he bit his tongue and counted to five. He finally asked quietly, "What's the matter?"

Helen sat down in her recliner and sighed. "My life is so boring. All I ever do is take care of the kids and cook and clean for you. We never go anywhere or do anything. We don't have any money to go shopping."

Ray was hurt. "I work all the time so we can afford this house and our standard of living. I'm sorry this life isn't exciting enough for you."

Helen struggled to her feet and pointed at him as she slurred, "I don't like your attitude—you're sleeping on the couch tonight."

Ray wanted to scream, but he just watched his unhappy wife stumble to their bedroom. He started to follow her and continue the argument, but he didn't because he thought of waking the girls. Ray slept on the couch that night and for the next three months until Helen moved out of the house and filed for divorce. Ray found out from mutual friends that she was dating Larry Alston, an older and wealthier attorney.

A year after the divorce, Ray started dating Amber. It was a fun relationship and the sex was amazing, but there was very little emotion involved. They were both busy people who enjoyed stress relief a couple of nights a week. Amber had informed him one night they were friends with privileges. Ray started to ask if she had any other friends with privileges, but thought better of it.

Sitting at the table, Ray finished his drink and then checked to make sure his doors were locked and turned out the lights. He went into his bathroom and relieved himself as he thought about Helen leaving him. He stripped down to his boxers and climbed into bed, underneath his down comforter. Caesar jumped up on the bed and lay down on top of the comforter, next to his feet. Ray fell asleep quickly and dreamed of his most vivid childhood memory.

** ** ** ** **

Ray's drunk mother yelled as he walked in the back door. "Raymond Caleb Harrison, I told ya not to go to the playground until you cleaned the yard. Just because you're in sixth grade doesn't mean you can't do your chores. Ya just wait 'til your dad gets home from work."

Ray's lips quivered as he pictured his drunken father stumbling in the door after beers with the boys. Ray took a step toward his mother as he pleaded with her, "Mom, I raked the yard before I left. Why are you mad?"

Ray's mother stood up from the kitchen table and slammed her glass of vodka on the table. "Ya didn't weed the garden. The weeds are chokin' my roses!"

Ray felt a lump in his throat. "But mom, I weeded last week."

Ray's mother walked up to her eleven-year-old son and grabbed him by the arms, shaking him. "Don't talk back to me! Do you understand? Don't talk back to me!"

Ray started to cry and his mom shoved him away. He ran to his room, slammed the door, and jumped onto his bed, crying until he fell asleep. Fortunately for Ray, his mother passed out before his dad came home.

Chapter 10

Wednesday morning, 8:51a.m.

Ray walked into the holding cell. "Good morning, Dallas."

Dallas was buttoning up his white pinpoint oxford shirt. "Mornin', counselor."

Ray looked at his watch, "Just a couple of minutes before the judge comes on the bench."

Dallas snickered.

Ray asked, "What's so funny?"

Dallas pointed to the walls with both hands, "We don't have clocks or watches or windows. The only way we know the time is at eleven at night when they turn off the lights and at six in the morning when the lights come on."

Ray hesitated. "Well, let's get an acquittal so we can get a watch back on your wrist."

Dallas nodded. "Sounds good to me. By the way, you really put that pompous old man in his place yesterday on cross-examination. I guess that's why they call you the killer lawyer."

Ray felt his face turn red. "I don't like being called the killer lawyer."

Dallas shrugged. "Sorry, I didn't mean to offend you. I would've killed the asshole, too."

Ray took a deep breath and forced himself to focus. "We've got the detective, the firearm expert, and FDLE people on the stand today. You did well yesterday by not showing any reaction when you got mad. Keep it up today."

Dallas nodded. "Sure thing."

Ray opened the heavy door. "The bailiff will bring you out in a minute."

Ray walked down the hall and nodded to the assistant bailiff at the entry to the courtroom, holding Dallas's belt. "I'm finished up. You can bring him out now."

The assistant bailiff walked back to the holding cell to supervise Dallas putting on the belt. Ray walked over to the defense table and arranged his file. Spere huddled with his paralegal at the State's table. A minute later the assistant bailiff brought Dallas into the courtroom and he sat down at the defense table. The head bailiff on the other side of the courtroom walked into the back room and let the judge know everyone was ready.

A few seconds later, the head bailiff stepped back into the courtroom and boomed, "All rise. The Honorable Gary Stalman is presiding over this court."

Judge Stalman decided to give the quick sitters a break and he said, "Be seated. Mr. Spere, call your first witness."

Spere stood up. "The State calls Brian Vetal."

The assistant bailiff opened the witness room and called his name. A burly, middle-aged man with salt and pepper hair and a goatee, dressed in a gray J.C. Penney's suit, walked in from the witness room and confidently stepped in front of the clerk.

After he swore to tell the truth, he sat down in the witness chair, and Spere asked, "Could you give us your name and rank?"

The witness leaned forward to the microphone and said in a deep voice, "My name is Brian Vetal, and I'm a detective with the Ft. Myers Police Department."

"Could you tell the jury how you became involved in this case?"

"I was the detective on duty when the report of a body at the Edison Home came in. I went over to the Edison Home and was talking to a witness when I received a call from an officer that heard the defendant threaten the victim the night before at the party. I met the officer at the station, and we prepared an affidavit and request for a search warrant. We took all of the information to the duty judge, and she signed the search warrant. We got two other detectives and went to the defendant's house to execute the search warrant."

"What did you see when you got there?"

The detective leaned back in his chair and used his hands to assist in his description. "The defendant's residence is a two story Spanish style house. There is a cement drive in the front and a black BMW sedan was parked near the front door."

"What did you do next?"

"We rang the doorbell, and the defendant answered wearing blue boxers and a white T-shirt."
"What did the defendant say?"

The detective hesitated for effect and looked directly at the jury. "He said, 'What's the matter? Did someone die?'"

An elderly female juror on the back row sat back in her chair and glared at Dallas.

Spere waited a few seconds before asking, "What did you say?"

"I told him we had a search warrant and read it to him. He kept interrupting me and asking what was going on."
"What did you do next?"

"I told him he could walk out to the patrol car and sit in the rear passenger seat voluntarily and be observed by an officer, or we could handcuff him and place him in the patrol car."

"What did he do?"

"He reluctantly went to the patrol car, but he was cussing like a sailor."

"What happened next?"

"Me and the other two detectives searched the house. We didn't find anything of significance, so we searched the BMW."

"Did you find anything of significance in the BMW?" The detective turned to the jury and raised his voice, "Yes, we found the murder weapon." "Where was the murder weapon?"

"It was slid underneath the driver's seat. I left it underneath the seat and called the crime scene techs to come collect the weapon for testing."

"What did you do next?"

"I walked over to the defendant and read him his Miranda rights."

"Did he agree to talk to you?"

The detective nodded. "Yes, he denied the gun was his and he claimed he'd never seen it before."

"Did you ever ask him about the argument?"

"Yes, I did. He started ranting and raving about the victim stealing money from him."

"At that point did you tell the defendant the victim had been murdered?"

"Yes, I did. I asked him why he killed Bryce Cervante." "What was his answer?"

"He claimed he didn't kill him." "What happened next?"

"I arrested him for murder and took him to jail." "No further questions."

Spere walked back to his table and sat down as Judge Stalman looked over at Ray and asked, "Cross-examination?"

Ray stood up and walked to the podium as he said, "Yes, Your Honor."

Ray looked at the detective and said, "Isn't it true, my client's fingerprints weren't on the murder weapon?"

"Yes, that's true. There were no prints on the weapon; it must've been wiped clean."

Ray was one step ahead of the detective. "Isn't it possible that the real killer fired the gun, cleaned her prints, and placed the gun in my client's car?"

The detective leaned back in his chair and scratched his chin, "Well, I guess it's possible. Just like it's possible I might hit the lottery tonight."

Two of the male jurors on the front row laughed quietly. Judge Stalman glared at them and they became stone-faced.

Ray asked, "Isn't it true the BMW was not locked?"

The detective stammered, "Um, I'm not sure."

Ray picked up some stapled papers from the podium, "Would it refresh your recollection to look at your report?" The detective shifted in his seat. "Uh, sure."

Ray looked at Judge Stalman. "May I approach the witness, Your Honor?"

Stalman nodded. "You may."

Ray walked up to the side of the witness box and showed the detective his report. As the detective flipped through his report, Ray could smell the detective's bad breath. He guessed the odor was either eggs with pepper and onion or an onion bagel with lox. Whatever it was made Ray step back a few feet until the detective looked up and handed Ray the report.

As Ray walked slowly back to the podium he asked, "Did that refresh your recollection?"

"Yeah, the car wasn't locked."

"Isn't it true there were no fingerprints on the driver's door handle?"

"Yeah, that's true, but that's not unusual. It's hard to get prints from a door handle."

"Isn't it also possible that the real killer wiped her prints from the handle?"

The detective had learned his lesson. "Yeah, it's possible."

"Did you perform a gunshot residue test on my client?"

"We did but it came up negative. We weren't surprised because it'd been a long time since the shooting, and he could've washed it off."

"You didn't find any bloody clothes either, did you?"

"No."

"No further questions."

Judge Stalman said, "The witness is excused. Call your next witness, Mr. Spere."

"The State calls Anita Bulger."

The assistant bailiff opened the witness room and called her name. A thirty something woman dressed in khaki pants and a blue polo shirt walked in from the witness room, stepped in front of the clerk, and swore to tell the truth. She sat down in the witness stand and looked up at Spere.

Spere said, "Please tell us your name and job title." "My name is Anita Bulger, and I'm a firearms expert for FDLE."

"Could you tell the jury about your experience with firearms?"

"Yes, my father was an avid hunter, so I grew up around guns. I got my college degree in mechanical engineering and I joined the Army for six years. While in the Army, I enrolled in a firearms inspection class after

92

basic training. I was assigned to the base quartermaster, and I inspected and tested all new firearms that arrived from the manufacturer. While in the Army, I completed two advanced classes in firearms safety and firearms engineering. After I was honorably discharged, I started working for FDLE as a firearms inspector. FDLE sent me to the FBI advanced firearms seminar at Quantico, and I take a seminar on firearms inspections every year in Tallahassee."

Spere looked up at the judge. "I tender Ms. Bulger as an expert in firearms."

Judge Stalman looked over at Ray. "Mr. Harrison?" Ray stood up. "No objection, Your Honor."

Judge Stalman looked back at Spere and nodded. "You may proceed."

"Ms. Bulger, did you receive a firearm related to this case?"

Ms. Bulger looked at her notes. "I received a sealed FedEx box with markings and a case number from the Ft. Myers Police Department. I opened the box and there were two sealed bags. One had a gun inside and the other had two bullets. They were both sealed with evidence tape and signed by the evidence tech from the police department. I logged them in and separated the bags."

"What did you do next?"

"I cut the bigger bag open with a pair of scissors and inspected the firearm with plastic gloves."

"What did your inspection show?"

Ms. Bulger looked back at her notes for a few seconds. "The serial number for the gun had been filed off. I looked inside the barrel and noticed a reddish-brown stain that appeared to be blood."

"What did you do with this stain?"

"I took a swab of the stain with a Q-tip and put it in a sealed plastic bag. I then sent it to the lab for testing."

"What did the testing of this stain show?"

"The stain was human blood, and it was a match with the victim's blood."

Spere hesitated and let the jury digest the significance, "What did you do with the second bag?"

"I cut the bag open and inspected the two bullets. They had obviously been fired. The attached report from the Ft. Myers Police Department stated they were recovered from a car seat that the victim was sitting in when found dead. The bullets appeared to be in the normal condition of bullets that had passed through a body."

Two of the female jurors on the front row looked at each other and shook their heads.

"Did you compare these bullets to the gun with the victim's blood in the barrel?"

"Yes, I did. I took the gun down to our gun range and fired a fresh bullet from the gun. I collected the spent bullet from the target on the range and took it to the lab with the other two bullets from the plastic bag."

"Could you tell the jury how you compare bullets to see if they've been fired from the same gun?"

The expert looked over at the jury, and they were on the edge of their seats. "It's really quite interesting. Every gun barrel has very small imperfections, and when a bullet is fired it turns rapidly as it goes through the barrel. The minutely small imperfections leave markings on the bullet that are unique to every gun. I took the bullet that I fired through the gun and compared it to the other two bullets under a microscope."

"What did you find?"

"I found that the bullets matched perfectly."

Spere nodded. "Based on your tests and your knowledge of firearms, did you form an opinion about the gun and the bullets that you examined?"

Ms. Bulger nodded and sat back in her chair. "Yes, I did. My opinion is the gun and bullets I examined were used to kill the victim. The grooves on the bullet fired in my lab matched the bullets taken from the seat. The fact there was blood spatter in the gun barrel tells me the gun was held next to the victim's skin when fired."

"What did you do with the gun and the bullets after you were done with the testing?"

"I put them back in their bags and resealed the bag with fresh evidence tape and signed the tape."

Spere walked back to his table and opened up a Bankers Box and took out a used FedEx box. He picked it up and asked, "May I approach the witness?"

"Yes, you may."

Spere walked up to the witness and handed her the FedEx box, "Could you open the box and pull out the contents?"

The witness pulled out two plastic bags and set them on the small counter in front of her that supported the microphone. She looked up at Spere.

"Do you recognize these bags?"

"Yes, I do. They have my markings on the tape, and I recognize the gun and bullets as the ones I examined."

"Your Honor, I request the gun and bullets be admitted into evidence."

Judge Stalman looked at Ray and he responded, "No objection."

Judge Stalman said, "They will be so received." Spere announced, "No further questions."

The judge looked over at Ray. "Cross-examination?"

Ray walked toward the podium with no notes as he said,

"Yes, Your Honor."

Ray stood at the podium and hesitated for three seconds before asking, "Could you tell the jury what a gunshot residue test is?"

"Yes. When someone fires a firearm there are microscopic particles emitted from the barrel that settle on someone's hand that fired the gun. A chemical test can be done to someone's hand to see if they have recently fired a gun."

"Isn't it true that my client didn't have any gunshot residue on his hands?"

"I don't know. I didn't do that test on your client." "No further questions."

Judge Stalman looked at Spere. "Redirect?"

Spere stood up. "Yes, Your Honor."

He walked to the podium and asked, "Isn't it true that gunshot residue can be washed off?"

"Yes, that's true. Over time it naturally fades over a twenty-four-hour period, but if someone were to vigorously wash their hands it could be scrubbed off."

"No further questions."

Judge Stalman looked over at Ray. "Recross?" "Yes, Your Honor."

Ray walked back to the podium and looked at the jury as he asked, "Don't you think it's unusual that a murderer could be sophisticated enough to wash away the gun shot residue and yet forget to hide the murder weapon?"

Spere jumped to his feet. "Objection, argumentative."
"Sustained."

"No further questions, Your Honor."

Judge Stalman looked at the jury. "We'll be in lunch recess until one o'clock."

Over the lunch break, Ray snacked on crackers and a diet coke in a corner of the law library while he mulled over the evidence. So far he evaluated the trial as a draw. All of the state's physical evidence had been admitted, and it was consistent with his theory and the state's theory. Theoretically, a tie goes to the defense, but Ray knew better. He needed a dramatic moment to shake the juror's preconceived notion of a police department arresting the right person. In every trial with a not guilty verdict Ray had been involved in, there was a dramatic moment when the jurors thought *maybe he didn't do it*.

Ray remembered three of his trials with dramatic moments that changed the momentum of the trial. The first trial was an armed robbery case where the victim stated to the police the person that robbed him was a black male about six foot tall and weighed 180-190 pounds. The robber wasn't caught that day. Three weeks later, Ray's client was arrested for beating up his wife's boyfriend when he came home early from work, and his mug shot accompanied the juicy story in the newspaper the next morning.

The victim of the robbery read the story and saw the picture. He immediately called the police and claimed he was the person that had robbed him. Ray's client was arrested for the armed robbery and hired Ray to defend him. Ray's client was adamant he didn't commit the robbery, so Ray took the deposition of the victim. During the deposition, Ray stood up and asked the victim, "Is the person that robbed you bigger than me, smaller, or about the same size?"

The victim eyed Ray up and down and said, "About the same size."

During opening statement of the trial, Ray talked about

97

how the entire case rises or falls based on the victim's identification of his client as the robber. He told the jury that the victim stated during his deposition that the robber was "about his size." Ray asked the judge if the defendant could be allowed to stand, so the jury could see his size.

The judge allowed it and the defendant stood up. Ray walked over and stood next to his client, who was eight inches taller and seventy-five pounds heavier than Ray.

Ray told his client to sit down, and he walked back to the podium where he told the jury, "They've got the wrong guy."

Three of the six jurors nodded. The case was over before the first witness testified. Even though the victim said he was 100% sure the defendant was the man that robbed him, the jury had their reasonable doubts. It was a five minute not guilty verdict.

The second example of a dramatic moment was a shooting case involving a police officer. Ray's client was accused of aggravated assault with a deadly weapon for allegedly trying to run over an officer with his car. The officer fired his gun nine times at the fleeing car, striking the defendant once in the back, paralyzing him. The defendant was jailed without bond, but he still sued the officer for excessive force within a month of his arrest.

At trial, the officer said he suspected the defendant was selling drugs in the convenience store parking lot. When he pulled in to investigate, the defendant got in his car and tried to drive away. The officer told him to stop, but he drove around the officer and attempted to flee the scene. The officer stated he was in fear for his life and that is why he emptied his clip in the defendant's car. The problem with his story was that two of the bullets were in the driver's side window and the remaining bullets were fired through the rear window. The bullet that paralyzed the defendant went through the back of the driver's seat and into his spine.

Ray's theory at trial was that the officer was angry at the defendant because he didn't obey his command to stop, and he fired his gun out of the anger, rather than protecting himself from the car being used as a weapon to crush him. Ray pointed to the location of the bullets to the side and rear of the vehicle to prove the officer was out of the path of the car. If it had happened the way the officer claimed, the bullets would have been in the front of the car. The officer claimed as he jumped out the way he fired his gun, and he fired the remaining bullets because other customers at the store could have been in danger. The officer had to blame the defendant to justify the shooting, or he would be liable for money damages in the civil lawsuit for excessive force.

It was eight months between the arrest and the trial. During that time, the officer had filed for bankruptcy and listed the defendant as a potential creditor because of the excessive force lawsuit. At the end of Ray's cross-examination of the officer he asked the officer, "Didn't you recently file bankruptcy?"

The officer growled, "Yes, I did. My wife ran up our credit cards and then left me for her old boyfriend."

Ray pressed. "Didn't you list the defendant as a creditor in your bankruptcy petition?"

The officer stammered a response, "Well, my, uh, bankruptcy lawyer said it was better to be safe than sorry."

Ray moved in for the kill. "Isn't it true, he told you he didn't believe your story of self-defense and knew you'd be held liable for the unlawful shooting?"

The officer's face flushed as he tried to think of a

response. He finally blurted out, "If your client had stopped when I told him to, we wouldn't be here today!"

The jury turned and looked at the defendant in a wheel chair. Suddenly, they considered the possibility that he hadn't tried to run over the officer, but was just fleeing the scene. It was a nineteen-minute not guilty verdict.

The third example was a case where Ray's client was accused of selling drugs to an undercover officer. The drug buy was videotaped, but it was poor quality and the hidden camera only gave a partial view of the transaction. The defendant was arrested a month after the undercover transaction and claimed he wasn't the person in the video. The police waited to make the arrest because the undercover officer's identity would be compromised. During this time period he did many other undercover buys. The prosecutor made a copy of the video for Ray and his client to view. Ray's client claimed it wasn't him, but Ray wasn't convinced. He told his client, the prosecutor would show the video only after the police officer pointed him out at trial as the person he bought drugs from. When this in-court identification was combined with the video, it was powerful evidence because jurors want to believe police officers.

The client was adamant it wasn't him, and even if it was, he didn't want to go to prison, so he insisted on a trial. Ray knew from experience that copies of video tapes were never as good as the original, so he made an appointment with the prosecutor to view the video at his office the day before trial. When Ray arrived for his appointment, the prosecutor was stuck in a hearing, so his secretary took Ray back to view the video in the media room with a younger prosecutor that was available.

There were no surprises while watching the

transaction, but the original video was not turned off after the transaction was completed. It kept playing while the undercover officer drove to a prearranged meeting place in a grocery store parking lot with the supporting officers that were monitoring the transaction via radio contact. When they got to the meeting place, the officers high-fived each other and said they were going to celebrate at a nearby bar. Of course, none of this celebration was mentioned in the police report and it was not on Ray's copy of the tape. The young prosecutor was amused, but didn't think it could hurt the State's case, so she never told the trial prosecutor.

The next day at trial, Ray was cross-examining the officer and asked him, "Isn't it true, you celebrated with the officers in the parking lot after the transaction and made plans to go to a bar afterwards?"

The officer replied indignantly, "Of course not. That would be unprofessional."

When the prosecutor played the tape, he turned the tape off after that drug transaction was completed. Ray convinced the judge that all of the tape should be played because the officer denied the celebration. The judge agreed and the entire tape was played. When the jury saw the celebration, they crossed their arms and glared at the prosecutor. It was a three minute not guilty verdict.

Ray knew he needed a dramatic moment in this trial to have a chance, and so far it hadn't happened.

Chapter 11

Wednesday afternoon, 1:03 p.m.

Ray had wanted to be a criminal defense lawyer since he watched his first episode of *Perry Mason* as a teenager. His parents weren't rich, so he knew he'd have to provide his own money for college and law school. During high school he worked as a bag boy at the local grocery store, and during college and law school he worked as a bartender. Between those jobs and student loans he was able to graduate with average grades. His law school advisor counseled him, "People who make A's make professor, people who make B's make judge, but people who make C's make money." Ray always remembered that advice in his early years as a struggling lawyer.

During Ray's law school years he was bored with all classes except criminal law, trail advocacy, and evidence. His evidence professor enjoyed challenging Ray's knowledge of the evidence rules. Every chapter had different examples illustrating the particular rule of evidence. One day the professor was lecturing about evidence that changes over time. The two examples in the text were blood and bodily fluids. They had to be refrigerated and sealed to protect their integrity as useful evidence. After the professor lectured on these two items, he looked at Ray and asked, "Can you think of any other evidence that might change over time?"

Ray contemplated the question for a few seconds before he smiled and answered, "Caterpillars."

* *   *   *   *

Judge Stalman had eaten spicy burritos for lunch, and he was in a foul mood. He walked into the courtroom, sat down at the bench, and looked up for a fast-sitter. He spied the pretty blonde TV reporter on the back row already bending her knees to sit down, anticipating his blessing to resume her seat. Judge Stalman waited until she sat down and boomed, "Ms. Fazig, everyone must rise when I enter the courtroom, even reporters."

Amber stood up quickly, embarrassed to be part of the story she was covering. She squeaked out, "I'm sorry." Ray turned and gave his lover a slight smile and rolled his eyes.

Judge Stalman waited two seconds and announced to the silent courtroom, "You may be seated."

After everyone sat down, Judge Stalman looked over at Spere. "Call your witness."

Spere stood up. "The State calls Ralph Marino."

The assistant bailiff opened the witness room and called his name. After he was sworn, Spere said, "Please give us your name and job title."

"My name is Ralph Marino, and I'm in charge of the evidence room at the Ft. Myers Police Department."

"Tell the jury what evidence was submitted to you on this case."

"I received three packages. One had a gun, one had two bullets, and one had blue rope with a yellow bungee cord."

"Can you tell the jury what you did with these packages?"

"The first thing I did was log them in on our intake sheet. I then stored them until the detective was ready for submissions."

104

"Tell the jury how the submissions worked in this case."

"Well, the detective showed up a few days after I logged them in and told me there was an arrest, so we needed to submit all of the evidence to FDLE. We submitted the two packages associated with firearms to one department at FDLE and the rope and bungee cord to a different department."

"Tell the jury the process of submitting evidence to FDLE."

"We sealed the packages inside a FedEx box and sealed the outside of the box with evidence tape and initialed the tape. We sent the secured FedEx boxes to the FDLE laboratory in Tampa. After they completed the tests, the results and items were returned to us."

"No further questions."

Judge Stalman looked at Ray and said, "You may inquire."

Ray approached the podium, "Sir, isn't it true that unless you have accurate history of an item, you have no way of knowing how an item was used in a crime?"

Marino thought about his answer for a second. "Everything we do is dependent on witnesses giving accurate info."

"No further questions."

Judge Stalman looked at Spere. "Call your next witness." "The state calls Joyce Napier."

The assistant bailiff opened the witness room and called her name. A petite woman in her late forties was sworn in by the clerk and sat down in the witness stand.

Spere asked, "Could you tell us your name and job title?"

Joyce answered in a strong Boston accent, "My name is Joyce Napier, and I work at the FDLE laboratory in

Tampa as lab assistant."

"What are your responsibilities as a lab assistant?"

"I'm responsible for receiving evidence submissions and keeping them organized for our scientists."
Spere opened another Bankers Box and pulled out a used FedEx box. He approached the witness as he asked, "I'm showing you State's Exhibit D. Do you recognize it?"

Joyce reached forward and took the box from Spere. She set it down on the counter in front of her and reached for her reading glasses in the front pocket of her light blue blouse. As she put the glasses on, she smiled up at Judge Stalman and said quietly, "My eyes aren't quite what they used to be."

Judge Stalman nodded, impressed that she acknowledged him in front of the crowd. He looked at her left ring finger and was pleased there was no jewelry. He made a mental note to call her after the trial when his wife was out of town. He lived by the zip code theory—it wasn't really cheating if you did it with someone from a different zip code.

Joyce looked at the package. "I recognize my handwriting on the evidence tape. I signed it in from the carrier and opened the box for testing the contents. After the testing was over, the scientist returned it to me and I put the items back in the box. I resealed it with evidence tape and initialed the top."

"No further questions."

Judge Stalman looked at Ray. "Cross?"

Ray stood up and shook his head. "No questions."

Judge Stalman looked down at Joyce and smiled.

"Thank you for coming down from Tampa. Stop by my office and my judicial assistant will sign your voucher to make sure you are reimbursed for your travel expenses.

Give her your contact information in case there's a problem with court administration getting you promptly paid."

She took off her glasses and beamed. "Thank you, Judge."

As she stepped down off the witness stand, Judge Stalman looked at Spere. "Call your next witness."

Judge Stalman enjoyed the rear view as Joyce walked out of his courtroom. Yes, he would definitely call her after the trial. He remembered why he liked having affairs with middle-aged women—they don't tell, they don't swell, and they're grateful as hell.

Spere stood up. "The State calls Joel Griner."

The assistant bailiff opened the witness room and called his name. A slim man with blue circular glasses walked in and was sworn in by the clerk. After he sat down Spere asked, "Could you give us your name and job title?"

"My name is Joel Griner, and I'm a scientist with FDLE."

Could you give us your educational background?"

Griner nodded. "I got my undergraduate degree, master's degree, and doctorate in chemistry from Georgia Tech."

Spere looked at Judge Stalman. "I submit Mr. Griner as an expert in his field."

Ray stood up. "No objection."

Judge Stalman nodded. "He will be so received and may render his opinion."

"What are your duties at FDLE?"

"I conduct tests on potential evidence left at a crime scene. My particular specialty is porous, non-metal items."

"Did you receive a rope and a bungee cord to examine in this case?"

Griner looked at his notes. "Yes, I did. There was a

fifteen-foot blue boating rope with a loop at one end and a three-foot yellow bungee cord. The police report stated they were used to secure the victim to a car seat and a steering wheel."

"What tests did you do on these items?"

"The first test we did was to check for biological fluids, such as blood, mucus, sweat, or semen. We are able to use this to determine the DNA of the person who left it. The victim's blood and sweat were on both the rope and the bungee cords. There were also some unidentified sweat molecules on the rope from someone other than the victim.

"The second test we did was to check the dye used to color the rope and bungee cord for any unusual characteristics we could use to trace the manufacturer, and potentially, which store sold the item. Unfortunately, the results were a common dye used by hundreds of manufacturers. Therefore, we were unable to trace the origins of the items."

"Were any other tests performed?"

"No."

"No further questions, Your Honor."

"Cross?"

Ray stood up and walked to the podium. "Sir, you mentioned some unidentified sweat molecules on the rope. Isn't it true, these sweat molecules didn't match my client's DNA?"

Griner smiled. "Yes, that's true. But someone that handled the rope in the past could have left the sweat particles. It's possible your client used gloves so he didn't leave evidence."

Griner gave Ray a smug smile. Because of the prior coached witnesses, Ray had anticipated Griner's rehearsed answer. Ray raised his voice in an accusatory tone. "Isn't it
108

just as likely the real killer left his sweat, and you haven't matched the real killer's DNA to the sweat sample?"

Spere jumped to his feet. "Objection, argumentative."

Stalman responded, "Overruled. Your witness suggested an explanation of the evidence, so he has opened the door to questions about alternative explanations."

Ray looked at the jury as he said, "Please answer the question."

Griner stammered, "Anything's possible."

Ray wasn't going to let him off so easy. "Please answer my question with a yes or no answer. Isn't it just as likely the real killer left her sweat and you haven't matched her DNA to the sweat sample?"

Griner was hard-headed. "No, that's not true."

Ray finally had Griner exactly where he wanted him. "Could you explain to the jury, statistically, how it's more likely that my client wore gloves rather than the real murderer left her sweat on the rope?"

Griner shifted in his seat and he hesitated before quietly answering, "I haven't performed any statistical analysis on this type of comparison. I'm not sure how it could be done."

Ray banged his hand on the podium. "Exactly. So let me ask the question one more time. Isn't it just as likely the real killer left her sweat, and you haven't matched her DNA to the sweat sample?"

Ray looked over at Dallas, and he was smiling.

Griner took a deep breath and realized he was a beaten man. "Yes."

Ray looked at the jury. An old Hispanic man in the back row slowly nodded his head. Ray happily announced, "No further questions."

Judge Stalman turned to the jury and said, "Ladies and

gentlemen, it's late in the afternoon. We're going to adjourn until nine in the morning; we'll see you then."

** ** ** ** **

Judge Stalman closed the door to his chambers and took off his robe. He grabbed a hanger from his full length coat rack and carefully centered his robe before hanging it back. He kept two other robes on the rack for backup. Every Friday he dry cleaned the robe he'd used that week. He always had a backup in case of a stain.

Judge Stalman had worked as a corporate lawyer at a large firm for ten years before he was appointed to the bench. His first five years on the bench he'd been a probate judge dealing with estate and guardianship cases. For the past twelve years he'd handled the criminal docket. His reputation among the criminal defense bar was that he would give the defendant a very fair trial. If the defendant was convicted, he would be given the maximum sentence. The defense lawyers had nicknamed him the "Time Machine" because of his harsh sentences.

Judge Stalman went to a judicial seminar his first year on the bench and absorbed all of the different theories on how best to run a courtroom. His favorite memory was an old retired judge that bragged at happy hour about giving out over 700,000 years in prison to different defendants over his career. He'd kept a weekly diary with all of the sentences he'd given out that week and added them up every year.

Judge Stalman was so intrigued by the story he vowed over his career to give out a million years in prison to deserving criminals. After all, everybody needed a goal.

110

Judge Stalman developed a quirky habit while he was in college. While many of his peers partied, he decided he wasn't going to waste valuable time that could be used for studying and making perfect grades. He forced himself to spend all his free time studying. One day during his freshman year he heard a friend describing his favorite football hero's DUI arrest. "He's a normal guy who got unlucky; he puts his pants on one leg at a time, just like us."

Stalman decided not to be like everyone else—he'd start putting his pants on both legs at once. It gave him a boost of confidence every morning knowing he was doing something different. He'd sit on the edge of his bed every morning and put his feet through both of his pants legs at the same time. He'd then slowly pull them up and lean back on his bed so they would come up evenly. It took longer, but he didn't care. He graduated with a 4.0 GPA, a degree in political science, and went to law school on a scholarship because he put his pants on two legs at a time.

Chapter 12

Wednesday afternoon, 5:42 p.m.

"I'll have a scotch and water," Ray said to the waitress at the Veranda.

Amber said, "Bring me a margarita and hold the salt."

As the waitress walked back across the brick patio Ray asked, "How'd you feel when Stalman called you out for sitting too quick?"

Amber sat up straight in her chair and growled, "That son-of-a-bitch. The other reporters warned me about him—he loves the limelight and showing off his power. He always told everyone to sit down once he walked on the bench. Next thing I know he's glaring at me and embarrassing me just for sport."

Ray was laughing so hard he snorted. It made Amber even madder and she warned, "Keep it up, funny boy, and you won't get any tonight."

Ray quickly calmed down his laughter, but he couldn't resist one last jab. "I saw the newspaper reporter in the elevator, and he told me he was putting your misfortune in hisstory."

Amber glared at Ray, "You're kidding!" Ray hesitated, "Well…yes, I am."

Amber was annoyed and abruptly stood up. "I'm going to the restroom."

As she stormed off, the waitress returned with their drinks. Ray grabbed his glass and drained half of it. Ray loved the first scotch of the day as it slid across his taste buds. He could feel the blood rushing to his tongue, stimulated by the alcohol waking his inner thirst. It reminded him of vampires in the movies when they saw a bleeding person. The wide eyes, the lust and the total satisfaction of the first blood of the night. He admired vampires because of their honesty—they knew they needed blood, and they didn't try to fight it.

Ray always felt guilty that he enjoyed alcohol. Both of his parents were alcoholics, and they died because of it while he was in college. After closing down a bar one night, Ray's father drove his truck into a canal and drowned. Two years after that, Ray's mother passed out on her couch after drinking vodka and smoking cigarettes all night. Unfortunately, her last cigarette was still lit and caught the couch on fire, burning down the house and killing her.

Ray drained his glass and signaled to the waitress for a refill. The French door from the inside of the restaurant opened, and Ray's investigator, Doug Shearer, walked out onto the brick patio. Doug was six feet even, with a barrel chest, trim waist, and he wore his light brown hair in a military crew cut. Ray waved him over and he nodded. Doug was wearing a yellow cotton button down with old jeans and topsiders. All of the women on the patio looked at Doug as he walked over to Ray's table and sat down.

"Good evening, counselor." "How're you doing, Doug?"

Doug motioned for the waitress. "I'm ready for a drink. I called all of my contacts today, trying to get you some good stuff for trial."

Ray leaned forward. "And?"

Doug held up his index finger. "I got you a few things, but let me get a couple of belts in first."

Ray understood and nodded. The waitress approached

114

with Ray's new drink and smiled at Doug. She sat Ray's drink down and said to Doug, "I remember you. You drink Patron gold over ice with lime."

Doug smiled. "You got it, honey. Bring me a double."

Doug saw Amber walking down the stairs, and he remembered the last time he'd seen her. A month before he was parked in a bar parking lot, hoping to catch a cheating husband with his lover and photograph them embracing in the parking lot. Unfortunately, the cheating husband was only drinking with the boys, and Doug was getting ready to call it a night. Then he saw Amber stumble out of the bar and wobble over to her car. Doug watched her fumble with her keys and they fell to the ground. When she bent over to pick them up, she tumbled over and sprawled out on the ground. Her purse had flung open and all of her stuff was spread out on the asphalt.

Doug got of his car and walked over to her. "Howdy, Amber. Had a little bit too much to drink?"

Amber started laughing. "Maybe, maybe not."

Doug reached down and helped her to her feet and she leaned against her car. He reached down, picked up her keys, and gathered everything back in her purse as he said, "How about I give you a ride home?"

Amber smiled and answered mischievously, "OK, Dougie. But remember, you've got to be nice to me."

Doug drove Amber home while he listened to her talk about her bad day at work and her unappreciative boss. He pulled into her apartment building and put the car in park. Amber looked over at him and said quietly, "Thanks for driving me home, Dougie."

She leaned over and hugged him, pulling him close. He quickly realized that it was more than a polite hug and felt his blood rushing to his face. Amber looked up and kissed him before he could say anything. He momentarily enjoyed her probing tongue, but broke off the kiss and pulled away from her. She looked surprised and hurt.

Doug said, "I can't. I'm friends with Ray."

Amber returned to her side of the car and gathered her purse. She didn't say anything as she got out of the car and walked around to Doug's window, bent over, and showed her abundant cleavage. Doug rolled down the window and Amber sultrily asked, "You sure you don't want to come up?"

Doug allowed himself to stare at her cleavage for a couple of second before he answered reluctantly, "Thanks, but I better not."

Amber straightened up and slowly walked away. As she reached the curb, she looked over her shoulder and purred, "Let me know if you ever change your mind. You can call me anytime."

** ** ** ** **

Amber walked up to the table and said in her best little girl voice, "Dougie, give me a hug. Ray's been mean to me."

Doug stood up and reluctantly hugged her. Amber positioned herself so she could watch Ray's reaction as she gave Doug a strong hug. Ray forced a smile after a few seconds and his right eye twitched. Amber was satisfied so she broke off the hug and said, "So Doug, tell me some good dirt I can use for a story."

Doug settled into his seat and stretched his arms to the side as he said, "Oh, let me think of something that you can sink your fangs into."

Amber sat down next to Ray and squeezed his thigh with her right hand as she grabbed her drink with her left. Doug leaned toward Amber and lowered his voice. "I was talking to a couple of my cop buddies earlier today about the trial. They got a memo from the chief of police about a new training seminar—how to act at trials. I guess they're pissed off that Ray embarrassed a couple of the officers during the trial. So, they're gonna have a seminar involving a mock trial and have some prosecutors act as judge and defense lawyer. They're gonna work on their performances like they're fucking actors. A lot of the boys are pissed off they gotta waste a day off on this baloney. They're thinking about filing a grievance with their union representative."

Amber cocked her head to one side and spoke slowly as she considered the story. "The teaser for the story could be COPS PRACTICE THEIR STORY or HOW COPS MANIPULATE JURORS."

Ray shook his head. "They don't need a seminar; the prosecutors just need to stop coaching the cops to say what they want."

They all took a hit on their drinks, and Ray looked at Doug. "Give me something I can use at trial."

Doug set his glass down. "I don't have a smoking gun, but I got a couple of things you can use. Remember the kinky shit on the victim's computer?"

Ray nodded, but then shook his index finger at Amber as he admonished her, "Nothing about this on the news until after the trial. I might use it, and I don't want the State to know that I know."

Amber didn't answer.

Ray raised his voice. "Nothing about this or no more exclusives."

Amber ground her teeth. "OK."

117

Doug continued, "The detectives finally got one of the victim's old girlfriends to talk about what he liked. This guy liked to be dominated and tied up by the woman. Apparently, it was his favorite way to get off."

Ray nodded, "So, are they gonna use this?"

Doug shook his head, "No. The woman clammed up and said she would never admit to it on the stand. Everything she said was off the record. The detective told me they went back to question her, and she's moved to the North Carolina mountains, but no one knows exactly where. Besides, how does that help them convict Dallas?"

Ray took another drink before he answered, "It doesn't—that's why they didn't follow up on it, or disclose it to me. Anything else?"

Doug shrugged his shoulders, "Nothing I can prove. But a lot of the cops are talking about Spere's black eyes. For the past couple of months everybody's wondering if Spere's wife might be slapping him around. Every time they ask him about the black eyes, he makes up ridiculous stories. A lot of the guys are talking."

Ray nodded slowly and said, "I've wondered myself." Amber said, "I couldn't do a story on that without proof. She'd sue us so fast if we didn't have confirmation from a third party."

Doug cracked his knuckles. "Enough about gossip. I want to hear how you think the trial is going."

Ray took a deep breath. "So far, so good. I'm still going with the theory that one of Bryce's sexual escapades went bad and someone, either the woman or her jealous husband, shot him."

Doug asked, "How are you gonna explain all of the evidence against Dallas?"

Ray smiled and shrugged. "It was all a setup."

118

Doug slowly shook his head. "Yeah, right. Someone was able to shoot Bryce and hide a gun in Dallas's car on the other side of town. How'd the killer know where Dallas lived and what car he drove? How'd the killer get Bryce in the Model T?"

Ray shrugged his shoulders. "I guess the jury is going to have to figure out the answers to those questions."

Amber reached under the table and ran her hand over Ray's thigh as she said, "People will never forgive you for sins they're dying to commit themselves, but are too scared to do."

Doug asked, "What do you mean by that?"

Amber lowered her voice. "Think about it. A lot of people hated Bryce, but they didn't kill him. I heard one of Bryce's buddies say that if Bryce ever patted you on the back, be careful because he was feeling where to put the knife. All of the jurors have hated someone at some time in their life—but they didn't kill them, because they didn't want to go to prison. These same jurors are looking at Dallas and thinking 'I know why you killed him, but I can't let you get away with it. I couldn't get away with it, and I'm not going to let you.'"

Ray whistled. "You've got some issues." Amber looked back and smiled. "You're right."

They all took a pull on their drinks as they considered Amber's analysis of the jury. Amber squeezed Ray's thigh underneath the table again. Ray realized Amber was ready to go and signaled to the waitress for his check. Doug looked around the patio for anyone listening and then said to Ray, "Anything else you need for me to do during the trial?"

Ray scratched his head. "Cervante's three ex-girlfriends are subpoenaed, and you've been in touch with them, right?"

"They're not happy, but if they don't show up for court we'll send a deputy to forcibly bring them to court. But they're not happy, so you better be careful what you ask them on the stand."

Ray countered, "You took their sworn statements right after Dallas's arrest, so if they try to change their story we can threaten them with a perjury charge."

Doug nodded and stood up. He drained his glass and said, "I've got to go down to Naples tonight and see an old girlfriend who's going through a divorce. I'll probably have to do a little charity work."

Amber rolled her eyes as Doug smiled mischievously. As the waitress walked over with the check, Amber waived goodbye to Doug as he left. As she set the check down, the waitress asked Amber, "Does your friend with the crewcut have a girlfriend?"

Amber blurted out, "Guys like him always have four or five. Maybe he can fit you into the rotation?"

The waitress walked away in silence and glanced back at Amber, trying to figure out her relationship to Doug. Ray pulled out his wallet as he said, "I guess I'll have to give her a good tip after that rude comment."

Amber gathered her purse as she said, "I wasn't being rude; I was just giving her the heads up on Doug. She'll thank me later."

Ray stood up and pulled back Amber's chair. She stood up and gave Ray a soft kiss on his cheek. He caught a whiff of her perfume, and he started to anticipate a pleasurable evening. They walked across the brick patio to the steps up to the French door, leading back into the piano bar. Ray held the door open and let Amber go in. As Ray walked in behind her, he heard a familiar voice from across the bar say sarcastically, "Check out the dynamic duo."

Ray turned to the baby grand piano and the six prosecutors sitting around it having drinks. He realized the comment had come from Spere, nursing a beer. Ray decided to be cordial. "How's it going?"

Spere was not in a sociable mood. "We're trying to figure out how you can sleep at night after defending murderers all day long."

Ray grabbed Amber's hand and pulled her towards the front door as he said, "I sleep like a baby after defending the wrongfully accused."

Spere sneered. "Yeah, right."

Ray and Amber walked toward the front door hand in hand. Spere looked at Amber and raised his voice as they reached the front door. "What does your boss think about you sleeping with a criminal defense lawyer to get a story?"

Amber looked back at the snickering prosecutors and the other curious patrons before she answered. "I get my stories from the courthouse. I'm sleeping with Ray strictly for pleasure."

** ** ** ** **

Amber came out of her bathroom dressed in a peach teddy and walked over to her stereo. Ray was nude in her king sized bed, relaxed between her red silk sheets, watching and anticipating her passion. She turned on a jazz station and lit three candles on her dresser. As she walked over to the bed, she whispered, "Did you miss me?"
Ray leaned toward her. "Yes."

Ray could feel his heart beating in his ears as Amber

lifted the sheet. As Ray anticipated her touch, her cell phone rang and she dropped the sheet as she walked over to her dresser to grab it, looking at the caller ID.

She walked back and sat down on the edge of the bed. She looked at Ray and said, "This is the station; I've got to get it."

Ray nodded and leaned back into her goose down pillow, biting his tongue. He wished he was home with Caesar. Whenever Amber would take her cell phone calls at night, Ray would go play with him. Ray had stopped by his house to let Caesar outside before coming over. As he walked out his front door, he heard Caesar whimpering.

Amber used her best telephone voice, "Hello."

Ray could hear a slight murmur through the phone for a few seconds. He turned over and pulled his pillow to his chest.

Amber replied, "No problem, Bill. I was just doing a little reading. Tell me what you need."

Amber listened.

After five seconds she said, "To find the footage, click under politics, and then click under commission meetings, then click under denials. That should get you the clip you need."

Ray listened to some more murmurs from the phone. "No problem; call anytime Bill. Have a good night."

She hung up and looked over at Ray. "I'm sorry. They needed some tape of one of the commissioners denying a conflict of interest with a developer. The developer just got indicted over in Miami on a bribery charge. They want to play the piece to stir up some shit."

Ray said, "Sounds like a good story."

Amber nodded and lowered her voice. "No more interruptions for the night, he promised."

Amber got under the sheet and snuggled up to Ray. As he put his arm around her and pulled her close she said, "I hope you aren't mad at me because I'm always on call."

Ray ran his hand down her back and stared into her eyes. "You're a twenty-eight-year-old thoroughbred and I'm a forty-five-year-old mule. I'm just glad to be along watching you win races."

Amber leaned into Ray and licked his neck as she pulled him close.

Chapter 13

Ray walked into the holding cell and Dallas asked, "What do you think about the rope and bungee cord testimony from yesterday?"

Ray ran his right hand through his hair as he considered his response. "I think it shows the police didn't do a thorough investigation. We can argue that he didn't struggle because he knew the person who tied him up—one of his girlfriends. Spere will argue you threatened Bryce with a gun, and therefore, he didn't struggle when you tied him up."

Dallas grabbed onto the bars and blurted out, "Why can't you tell me something good?"

Ray shrugged his shoulders. "I can lie to you if you want and guarantee everything's going to be OK." Dallas pleaded, "At least tell me something good."

Ray nodded. "I can do that. All of the TV stations and newspapers are saying it could go either way. Hopefully, the jury feels the same way."

Dallas sat down on the stainless seat and leaned against the cement wall. He lowered his voice. "I know you're doing your best, but it's scary in here. Some of the inmates want to beat me up, or worse, because I'm in the news. They can grab some notoriety in the jail by getting a piece of me."

Ray grabbed the bars and leaned as close as he could. "I'm gonna do everything I can to get you out of here, Dallas. I promise."

Ray turned and walked back toward the heavy door, "They'll bring you out in a minute."

** ** ** ** **

After Dallas was booked in for murder on the first floor of the jail, the jailers moved him to the fourth floor with the other high-risk inmates. The fourth floor of the jail was made up of accused murderers, rapists, kidnappers, and other sexually deviant criminals.

The fourth floor of the jail was divided up into two sections. Each section had a large open area, cheerfully called the day room, where inmates could mingle, read, play cards, or watch the one available TV. Many fights had occurred over who had control of the TV remote. The jailers still talked about one memorable fight over the TV remote.

One section housed four members of a gang, and they controlled the remote. They kept the TV tuned to rap videos from six in the morning until lights out at 11:00 p.m. After a week of listening to the rap music, a large redneck grabbed the control and switched to a fishing show. He refused to switch the show, so the gang members attacked and beat the redneck until he passed out.

They changed the TV back to rap music videos and then rammed the remote up the rectum of the unconscious redneck. When he finally woke up, he had to be taken to the hospital to have the remote surgically removed. There was a rumor that the hospital made a video of the procedure and still showed it to new interns.

At 11:00 p.m. the day room got cleared, and all of the inmates were forced into their assigned small cell with a bunk bed they shared with another inmate. The cell doors were electronically locked from the shift supervisor's office from 11:00 p.m. until 6:00 a.m. At that time, the locks were remotely released, and the inmates could move to the day room if they desired. Each section was taken to the cafeteria for their daily meals separately.

When Dallas was taken to the fourth floor of the jail, the jailer escorted him to his cell and introduced him to his cellmate, Julio Sanchez, sitting on the lower bunk. Julio was six foot and a muscular 350 pounds. He'd gotten a jailhouse tattoo of a spider web on his shaved head. The apex of the web was at the crown of his head and it extended 360 degrees down to his ears and eyebrows. Jailhouse tattoos were a tradition carried on by inmates pricking themselves with staples, or paperclips, and then coloring the open wounds with black pens.

After the jailer left the cell, Julio asked Dallas, "Do you want to be the wife or the husband?"

Dallas quickly thought of the pros and cons of each position in jail. After a few seconds of panicked reasoning he stammered, "I guess I'll be the husband."

Julio nodded and then smiled slightly. "Come over here and suck your wife's dick."

Dallas ran out of the holding cell into the day room. All of the inmates and jailers standing outside the day room bars were laughing. Dallas stood in the middle of the room, angry at being the butt of the joke, and determined not to be in the cell with Julio. Julio stepped out of his cell and waived. He motioned for Dallas to come back in and the laughter intensified.

After the laughter calmed down, the shift supervisor yelled through the bars to Dallas, "Don't give us any trouble, or we'll lock you in the cell overnight with Julio.

Your real cell is two doors to the right of Julio's; we let him have his own cell most of the time. But you should know about six months ago we had this problem inmate here named Sebastian. We locked him overnight in the cell with Julio. The screams were so bad no one on the entire floor got any sleep that night.

"The next morning we had to take ole' Sebastian to the hospital. He ended up staying about three weeks, and the day he came back to jail he called up his public defender and said he wanted to plead to his manslaughter charges and take the thirty-year plea offer. He really wanted to get out of our jail and go to prison. Of course, there are dozens of men like Julio in every prison, but I guess Sebastian hoped they'd be more gentle."

** ** ** ** **

As Ray walked down the hallway to the courtroom, he wondered what it must be like to be locked up, depending on the wisdom of twelve strangers to set you free. He walked back into the courtroom and the steady hum of talk from the spectators and court personnel. As he walked back toward the defense table, he passed by Spere unloading his briefcase. He looked closely at his face for signs of a hangover from the night before. Spere looked up at Ray and nodded. Ray noticed he had a black left eye and he said, "The wife slap you around last night for coming in late?"

Spere glared at Ray. "I walked into a door last night. Not that it's any of your business."

Ray smiled widely and used his best condescending voice, "Yeah, right."

The bailiff announced, "All rise, Judge Stalman is presiding over this court."

Judge Stalman walked in and sat down. "Please be seated."

After everyone sat down and got comfortable in their seats, Judge Stalman looked at Spere. "Call your first witness."

Spere announced, "The State calls Harry Talbot."

The assistant bailiff opened the witness room and called his name. A short, stocky man walked in dressed in his Sunday best. The clerk swore him in, and he quickly settled into the witness chair and looked at Spere.

"Give us your name and what you do for a living." "My name is Harry Talbot, and I'm an assistant to the medical examiner."

"What does an assistant to the medical examiner do?" "I help the drivers transport bodies and transfer them to the examination room at the morgue. I also assist the medical examiner during the autopsy. I take pictures of the body and any evidence recovered from the body. After the exam, I prepare the body for release to relatives."

"Did you transfer a body from the Edison Home on January eighteenth of this year?"

Talbot nodded. "Yes, I did. The driver and I cut the blue rope holding the body to the driver's seat in the old car and untied the yellow bungee cord. We then covered the body with a privacy tarp and secured it to a wheeled stretcher. We then transported it to the morgue for the autopsy."

"When you moved the body from the car seat, what happened?"

Talbot took a deep breath and lowered his voice. "When we moved the body there was a lot of coagulated blood caked on the seat and the floorboard. When we untied the body, patches of semi-dried blood fell off the seat and we could see two bullets lodged in the car seat. We showed the detectives and then moved the body to the transport vehicle."

"No further questions."

Judge Stalman asked, "Cross-examination?"

Ray walked toward the podium, unsure of a few quick questions or an extensive cross-examination. He glanced at the jury and saw one woman and three men holding their hands over their mouths. He decided to gamble and ask a question to which he didn't know the answer. "Did you notice anything unusual about the body?"

Harry shifted in his chair and looked up to his left, searching his memory. "Well, now that you mention it, there was an unusual smell around the victim's neck and chest. It smelled like jasmine."

Ray felt a chill go from his ears, down his neck and settle in the base of his spine. He stared at Talbot and said nothing for a full five seconds. He felt sweat forming on his brow.

Finally, Judge Stalman brought him out of his trance, "Any more questions, Mr. Harrison?"

Ray cleared his throat. "This jasmine smell, did it smell like cologne, or maybe, perfume?"

Harry nodded his head. "Yes, that's what it smelled like. It was a weak smell that I could only smell when I was close, wrapping the body with the tarp."

Ray stammered, "I have no other questions, Your Honor."

Judge Stalman announced, "Call your next witness." Spere stood up. "The State calls Jocelyn Carter."

The assistant bailiff opened the witness room and
130

called her name. A tall woman in her fifties walked in carrying a file and was sworn in by the clerk. The lady settled into her chair and opened her file.

Spere said, "Give us your name and job title."

"My name is Dr. Jocelyn Carter, and I'm the local medical examiner."

Spere went through her educational background and her work experience. He then proceeded to go through the details of the autopsy with his witness, complete with a slide show of the body being cut up and examined. Ray had warned Dallas ahead of time to look down and not look at the pictures. An innocent man would be horrified seeing pictures of an autopsy. A guilty man might be curious of looking at his prize one last time. Ray knew the autopsy proved nothing except that a man died because of two bullets passing through his heart. The real reason the prosecutor put the medical examiner on the stand was to remind the jury of the murder, show them gruesome pictures, and let them take their outrage out on the only person in front of them—the defendant.

After Spere finished his direct examination, Ray went to the podium for cross-examination.

"Isn't it true, there were no signs of struggle on the defendant's body before he was shot?"

"That's true."

"Can you tell the jury how you look for signs of a struggle?"

"We look for broken fingernails, defensive wounds to the arms or hands, and bruising."

"Isn't it true, there were none present in this case?"

"That's true."

"No further questions."

As Ray returned to his seat, Judge Stalman announced,

"We'll take a lunch break until one o'clock."

Chapter 14

Thursday noon

After the courtroom cleared out, Ray met Amber and Doug in the lobby, next to a large window. Ray asked them, "What do you think?"

Amber answered, "It was a woman that killed Cervante. No man would wear jasmine cologne; that means a woman left her scent. It also explains why there were no wounds from a struggle or defensive wounds—he let himself be tied up by some kinky freak."

Ray started to say his ex-wife wasn't a kinky freak, but he thought better of it. He nodded and looked at Doug. "What about it?"

Doug scratched the back of his neck. "I agree with Amber. But how do you pick up some chick and talk her into that sort of thing at a formal party?"

Amber said matter-of-factly, "Some guys are persuasive if they've got the right equipment."

Ray and Doug looked at Amber in amazement. Amber blushed and shrugged her shoulders. "Some guys have a gift."

Ray wondered how extensive Amber's research was to justify her opinion.

Doug said, "That also explains why he's naked. I know if a woman ever asks me to get naked, the answer is yes."

Amber and Doug laughed, but Ray was still preoccupied thinking about Amber's research methods as he looked out the window. As Ray looked out the window, Amber looked over at Doug and raised her eyebrows. Doug avoided her inquisitive look and stepped up to the window and followed Ray's glance to the smokers gathered in the smoking area.

Amber snapped her fingers. "That explains the bullets to the heart; she gets a two for one special. She kills the guy and makes a statement—you broke my heart, so I'll break yours."

Doug shook his head, "I don't know about that; I think she just wanted him dead. If she wanted to make some kinda statement she coulda done a Lorena Bobbitt on him."

Ray considered Doug's theory. "Ouch."

Amber said, "I don't know the details, but I think we all can agree it wasn't Dallas."

Ray answered, "I hope the jury feels the same."

Amber looked at Ray, "I've got to go to the doctor this afternoon. I've been feeling bad the past couple of days. I'll call you after that. Plan on coming over tonight. I'm going to cook spaghetti."

Ray smiled. "Sounds like a plan. I'll talk to you later."

As Amber walked off, Doug asked, "If you don't need me this afternoon, I'm gonna do some other stuff. My other clients are yelling and screaming for me to work on their cases"

Ray shook his head slowly, "I can't think of anything. If I do, I'll call you on your cell."

As Doug turned and started to walk away he said, "No problem. You know it's on 24/7."

Ray nodded and pulled his cell phone out of his pocket as Doug walked down the hallway. He saw Helen had called five times in the past hour, so he dialed her number. He definitely needed to talk to her.

Helen picked up on the first ring, "Hello, Ray."

Ray said politely, "Hey, I saw where you called a
134

bunch of times. What's up?"

"Beth got caught with pot in her purse at school today."

Ray's anger made him gasp for air. "What? How long has she been smoking pot?"

"I don't know. It surprised me, too."

Ray tried to settle down before he continued. "So, what happened?"

Helen's tone turned to indignation. "I guess one of her so-called friends told the principal, and he searched her purse. They suspended her, so I went and picked her up. I restricted her to her room until we talked."

Ray held back his anger and said in an even tone, "Talk to her when you've both settled down, and take her to a counselor for an evaluation."

"That sounds good to me. How's the trial going?"

Ray hesitated and took a deep breath before he plowed ahead. "There was some interesting testimony today from the medical examiner's assistant. He testified that when he moved the body he smelled a jasmine scent."

Helen didn't answer for a few seconds. She finally said quietly, "It's a very popular perfume."

Ray took a deep breath and said forcefully, "Yesterday, I got to see the blue rope and yellow bungee cord in person. Before trial, I only saw a black and white copy of a photograph of them. In person, they looked very similar to the ones you keep in your Suburban for the jet skis and hauling antiques."

Helen was quiet for five seconds before she asked, "What are you saying, Ray?"

Ray raised his voice, "You were at the fundraiser. Who were you with when Bryce was murdered?"

Helen replied icily, "I was with my husband." Ray asked forcefully, "Did you kill Bryce?"

Helen hesitated for few seconds before answering in an even tone, "Your children love you."

Ray heard a click and then silence.

** ** ** ** **

Helen placed the cordless phone in its charger and unplugged the line from the phone jack. She didn't want Ray to call back and leave an incriminating message on the answering machine and have her husband listen to it. For the prior two years Larry had watched her like a hawk— checking the call history, and messages on the house phone and her cell phone. He never let her forget about her affair, not even one day.

Larry had hired a private investigator two years before and caught Helen with her boyfriend—Bryce Cervante, his law partner. Cervante & Alston had been a high profile law firm for twenty years, so when the firm broke up, the secretaries made sure they told all of their friends about one partner's wife sleeping with the other. The downtown gossip mill had it all over town within a day. Everyone remembered Helen and Ray had divorced three years before, and that was because of her affair with Larry. Many people relished that Larry got what he gave.

Unbeknownst to Larry, Helen had told Bryce she'd get divorced if she could move in with him. Bryce said he wasn't the marrying type, and Helen stayed with Larry because she had no other immediate option. When she married Larry, she lost her alimony payments from Ray. Larry had insisted on a pre-nuptial, so she would have peanuts if she left Larry without another man to support her in the style to which she was accustomed. Helen was no longer in love with Larry, but she needed him financially, although she hated it. Larry was determined to stay married, and Helen agreed to go to counseling.

Helen remembered their first meeting with the counselor after the affair. After the preliminary introductions, the counselor broke the ice. "Let's start with you, Larry. Tell me why you're here."

Larry couldn't resist. "Because she started fucking my law partner."

Helen's face turned crimson, but she said nothing. The counselor hesitated, glancing at Helen and back at Larry before he said sternly, "We can't change the past or forget it. However, the one thing we can do, or not do, is forgive. I assume both of you are here because you want to salvage your marriage. Is that correct?"

Helen thought *I'm here because I need this tired old ride until I can trade up to a newer model,* but she said quietly, "Yes, I was wrong. I love you, Larry; I want to make this work."

Larry let his guard down and took a deep breath. He was mad, but he knew he still loved Helen, and didn't want to lose her. He said softly, "I want to work through our problems. But I can't handle this ever happening to me again."

Helen thought *it won't happen again, because I'm not coming back after my next affair,* but she wiped away an alligator tear as she whispered, "I'm so sorry I hurt you."

They continued in counseling for six months, and the home life returned to normal, except for Larry's suspicion. He'd call Helen a dozen times a day on her cell, and checked her cell history at home. He'd try to be discreet and check it when Helen was in the shower. Helen found out one day when she was running bath water. She turned the bath water off and used the commode, taking the last of the toilet paper. She looked under the sink and realized she was out. She put on her robe and walked to the garage to get a package of toilet paper off the shelf. As she walked by the kitchen, she saw her husband from behind, checking her cell phone. She was angry, but didn't confront him.

After her shower, she put on her robe and walked into the kitchen, pouring a glass of iced tea. Larry was sitting at the breakfast table, eating a sandwich and watching the kitchen TV. He looked up and asked, "Have you heard from Susie since she moved to Key West?"

Helen thought *asshole, checking my calls*, but said, "Yeah, she called the other day to say she was homesick. She likes her job, though."

Larry nodded, "Sometimes the grass isn't greener on the other side."

Helen thought *most of the time it is*, but said, "You're right on that, honey."

Larry smiled and took a bite of his sandwich.

Helen was ready to make a move, with or without a new man. She decided she wanted to be a real estate salesperson, so she enrolled in school and studied every night for two months. Larry was not happy about her new venture, but figured it wasn't all bad because she didn't have time to have another affair. But just to make sure, he checked her cell phone every morning for any unfamiliar numbers.

Helen finally graduated from real estate school and began studying for the state exam. She asked her husband about potential real estate firms, and he sent her to a former client, Dallas Kelley. She called and made an appointment to meet with Dallas. Dallas was impressed with her enthusiasm and potential referral base from her husband's firm. He hired her to work as his assistant until she passed
138

her state exam and got her license.

On her third day on the job, she walked into Dallas's office. "Hey, I got a great lead. One of Larry's clients is a rancher out in LaBelle. They met this morning and he told Larry he was ready to sell out and retire. He just called me and wants to list 100 acres."

Dallas sat up in his chair and quickly did the calculation: acreage was selling for $100,000 per acre multiplied by 100 equaled a sales price of ten million dollars. The real estate commission on vacant land was ten percent—a one million dollar payday when it sold. Dallas smiled and said sweetly,
"Good job. I'll have it sold within thirty days to this developer I know from Lauderdale."

Helen asked, "How much of the commission will I get?"

Dallas stammered, "Well, you haven't passed your exam yet, so I can't legally give you any of the commission."

Helen's face twitched. "That's bullshit! I brought this guy here."
Dallas put up his hands in a surrender posture. "Hold on. Don't get mad; we can work something out." Helen blurted out, "Like what?"

Dallas's mind was in fast forward with the calculations as he spoke, "I've got to pay taxes on the million dollar commission. That leaves six hundred and fifty thousand or so. All of the overhead takes off another fifty thousand. How about I give you $100,000 cash in a paper bag when the deal closes?"
Helen started doing her own calculations. After three seconds, she smiled and announced quietly, "You got a deal."

Dallas was correct about his Ft. Lauderdale developer wanting the property—he had a contract within three days of listing the property. The closing was scheduled sixty days after the contract was signed. During this time, Helen brought two other listings into the office. They were both riverfront homes listed in the seven figures. Dallas promised Helen ten percent of his fee, in cash, after closing on each of the properties.

Dallas invited Helen and Larry over to his house for dinner one night to celebrate all of the new listings. Dallas had it catered with filet mignon, champagne, and caviar. Dallas and his young blonde girlfriend entertained them with stories of their latest European vacation. Helen was excited with her new career and financial independence. She started planning on divorcing her husband and getting her own place. She continued studying for her real estate exam. Three days before her big payday on the ranch closing, she took the real estate exam and flunked it.

The next day she walked into Dallas's office and her voice cracked as she said, "I failed the exam."

Dallas carefully weighed his reaction. He didn't want anything to upset the ranch closing and his million dollar fee. He spoke in the best compassionate voice he could muster, "It's OK, Helen—a lot of people fail it a few times. It's no big deal; you just gotta dust yourself off and take it one more time."

Helen plopped down in a chair. "Really?"

Dallas nodded. "Hell, I flunked it the first time. I can point to three of the biggest producers in the county that flunked it three or four times. Nobody cares once you get your ticket and start making money."

Helen felt slightly better. "I still have my job, right?"

Dallas smiled and lied, "Of course."

Helen thanked him and walked back out to her desk. Three days later Dallas went to the title company for the closing on the ranch property. He came back to his office with a check for one million dollars. As he walked in the front door, Helen rushed toward him and blurted out, "Did it close?"

Dallas smiled. "Yes."

Helen jumped in the air. Dallas motioned with his finger, "Let's go back to my office."

Helen nodded and followed like a two-month-old puppy.

Once inside his office with Helen, Dallas said, "I've got to go to the bank and deposit the check. It'll take a day for the funds to clear. I'll get you the cash tomorrow afternoon, Okay?"

Helen gushed. "Of course, that's fine."

Dallas smiled and said sweetly, "Go ahead and take the rest of the afternoon off. I'll see you tomorrow morning." Helen beamed. "Thank you."

She walked over and gave Dallas a full frontal hug and squeezed.

After a couple of seconds, Dallas stepped back from the intense hug and gave her a polite smile. "Enjoy the afternoon."

Helen was slightly taken aback; no man had ever ended a hug before she was ready. She looked inquisitively at him, and Dallas motioned toward the open door. "A lot of nosy people."

Helen nodded. "Oh, okay"

She stepped toward the door and looked back tentatively. "Well, I guess I'll see you tomorrow." Dallas smiled. "You bet."

Helen went home and quickly got on the internet. Over

the next three hours, she researched web sites for apartments, cars, designer clothes, travel, and divorce web sites. Larry called her a dozen times on her cell phone, but she allowed voice mail to pick up. She didn't care if he was angry, and gave her the third degree, because her days in the house were numbered. When he came home later and confronted her, she started a fight that ended with Larry being told he was sleeping on the couch.

The next morning Helen woke up completely rested and excited. She made it to work the next morning at 8:55 a.m., surprising everyone because she had never been early before. When she walked in, she noticed the office was extraordinarily quiet. As she walked to her desk, no one would look at her. She sat her purse down on her desk and noticed an empty Bankers Box on the edge of her desk. Dallas stepped out of his office and motioned for her.

She walked into his office and saw two armed security guards standing behind Dallas's desk. Helen looked at the guards and back at Dallas. "What's going on?"

Dallas said, "Have a seat, Helen."

She sat down on the edge of her seat. "What's going on?"

Dallas sat down in the chair behind his desk and cleared his throat. "Helen, I'm sorry to say that I'm going to terminate your employment. You've flunked the real estate exam, and I need to hire someone that can help me on my sales."

Helen's head started spinning. "What? You said it was no big deal that I flunked the exam."

Dallas shook his head and said fervently, "I don't know what you're talking about."

Helen yelled, "What the fuck are you talking about?"

Dallas glanced at the guards. "Helen, there's no need to
142

use profanity. Please, clear out your desk, and these gentlemen will escort you to your car."

Helen screamed, "Where's my money?"

"The book keeper will send you your paycheck for this week and two weeks severance pay."

Helen slammed her hands on Dallas's desk. "Where's my $100,000?"

"I don't know what you're talking about, Helen."

Helen couldn't breathe, and her blood was pounding in her ears. She finally remembered to breathe and hissed, "You motherfucker! Where's my money?"

The security guards stepped forward. The older one motioned towards the door, "Ma'am, you need to leave. Clear out your desk, and put your personal belongings in the box. You must vacate the premises."

Helen stood up and the security guards stepped toward her. She pointed at Dallas and yelled, "I'm going to get my money, you piece of shit."

Helen stormed to her desk and loaded up the Bankers Box and walked to her car with the guards two steps behind. As she drove off, she started thinking about her lost money. She'd already decided on which apartment she was going to rent, and which convertible she was going to buy. No $100,000, no job, no divorce, no independence, nothing but her old jealous husband at home. She started thinking about suing Dallas, but realized he was three steps ahead of her. There was no written contract about the kickback, and the security guards were witnesses who would confirm that Dallas denied ever knowing about any kickback. And of course, the icing on the cake, her flunking the real estate exam would be a legitimate reason to justify her firing.

Helen drove home and unloaded her personal belongings: a framed 8"x10" of her two daughters at the beach, a laptop computer, study aids for the real estate exam, and her notary stamp. She opened a bottle of wine, and sat down on her comfortable leather couch, and watched the morning talk shows. She had emptied the first bottle, and was half way through the second when her cell phone rang. Sure enough, Larry was calling to check on her. She answered and told him she got fired because she flunked the state exam. She'd never told him about her cash kickback because that was her go-away money.

Larry was secretly pleased over his wife's firing. She'd been preoccupied with her new career and always told him she was tired at night when he snuggled up to her in bed. In the past, she'd always been content to be a stay-at-home mom. Larry had always paid for a maid, and they ate out almost every night. Helen went to the gym daily and a salon for her weekly pedicure and manicure. She enjoyed shuttling her daughters to all of their activities. Things in the bedroom had slowed down since the affair, but they had gradually made a comeback, at least until her new career. Maybe now she would go back to her normal routine and be more attentive to him.

For the next two months, Helen went back to her old routine, but she wasn't happy about it. She told Larry she was tired of his snoring, so she began sleeping in the spare bedroom. Larry was livid and bought every snoring aid on the market. This amused Helen because she'd lied about the snoring—it was an excuse to avoid him in the bedroom.

Helen was ready to leave Larry, but she was too depressed to take the real estate test a second time, so she started thinking of other options. One day at the gym she borrowed a girlfriend's cell phone and walked outside for privacy. She called Bryce and suggested they meet at his house for a nooner. He eagerly accepted.

144

After a rigorous session of sex, they were relaxing in bed, arms and legs intertwined, when Helen whispered, "I've got to leave Larry. I'm sick of him."

Bryce asked, "What can I do?"

"I need some money to get set up in an apartment." "Let me talk to a friend that has a complex and see if there are any openings. I'll call you tomorrow."

"No, don't call me—he checks my call history. I'll call you tomorrow afternoon."

"Okay."

Helen lifted her head up and whispered in Bryce's right ear, "Thank you."

Helen rolled Bryce onto his back and thanked him with the rest of her body. She showered and got dressed while Bryce jumped in his pool nude and swam some laps, his privacy protected by a ten-foot hedge along his property line. She walked out on the patio and gave Bryce a goodbye kiss as he was drying off.

As Helen was walking away Bryce said, "Helen, I miss you. We had something special."

Helen looked back over her shoulder and said coyly, "I'll call you tomorrow." After she got back in her car, she checked her cell phone and saw Larry had called her four times within a two hour period. She called him back and said she'd been at the gym and left her cell in the car. Larry reminded her the counselor had told them they needed to communicate. She bit her tongue, took a deep breath, and apologized.

The next day she called Bryce from the gym phone, but he wasn't in. She left a message with his secretary and told her she'd call back later. She called three times the rest of the day from different phones, but Bryce was never available. She called the next morning from the gym and

Bryce's secretary answered the phone, "Hello, law office of Bryce Cervante."

"This is Helen. Is Bryce in?"

The secretary stammered, "Um, well he's with a client. But, he asked me to give you a message: He can't help you with your problem."

"Excuse me?"

The secretary said firmly, "He told me to tell you he can't help you with your problem."

Helen hesitated for a few seconds and growled, "Son of a bitch."

She hung up the phone and started hitting the pillow on her bed. After beating the pillow into submission, she put her face in it and started to cry. Thirty minutes passed before she was cried out. She rolled over in her bed and started thinking about her options. She decided she was going to take the real estate exam again. After she passed it, she would start working and make her own money. Meanwhile, she would sleep in a separate bedroom and spend a lot of time with her daughters.

Helen's schedule for the next six weeks was regimented. She'd wake up at 6:00 a.m. and make sure her daughters were fed and at the bus stop on time. She'd pack her gym bag and give her husband a quick peck on the cheek on the way out the door. After a workout at the gym, she'd grab a late breakfast at the Oasis restaurant downtown. After a hearty meal, she drove a short distance to the public library. She started going to the library to get away from her husband and the distraction of phone calls and TV at home. She'd study until three in the afternoon and head home. She'd meet her daughters and shuttled them back and forth to ballet practice, soccer games, and swim practice. After her daughter's last practice, she'd call

146

ahead to a restaurant and order takeout.

After a family dinner, she'd clean up and allow herself an hour of TV with her daughters. After her daughters were in their bedroom, she'd go to the living room and turn on all the lights before she began her evening study session. She made sure the study session lasted until her husband went to sleep in their bedroom. Only then would she turn off the lights and go to sleep in the spare bedroom.

After six weeks of her own boot camp, Helen took the real estate salesman exam for the second time. She flunked it again. She was very depressed, so she started watching a lot of TV and having a food orgy with Sara Lee and Ben & Jerry.

After a week of depression, Helen started thinking of what her new plan might be. She decided she was going to look for new husband prospects. The annual Edison Historical Society Ball was the following weekend, so she went shopping in Naples and found a low-cut purple gown that fit her perfectly. She spent the next three days shopping for shoes that matched.

On the day of the fundraiser, she started early at the salon with a facial, manicure, and pedicure in the morning. After a light lunch, she went back to have her hair styled and put up in a formal fashion to go with her gown. She went home and relaxed in a nice long bubble bath. She drank a couple of glasses of wine as she did her makeup and got dressed.

When Helen walked into the living room, her husband lavished her with compliments. However, she didn't need the compliments; she knew she looked good. On the way to the gala, her husband bored her with his latest case about the permitting laws and his non-compliant client. She started thinking of how she could politely ditch her husband without him being suspicious. She settled on the old standby of steering him toward his golfing buddies and letting them tell stories of their latest dramatic golf shots. She could slip away and look for someone interesting.

As they were walking up to the giant Banyan tree at the Edison Home, Helen saw Bryce and Dallas pushing each other and yelling. A crowd gathered quickly and she could barely see through it, but she was able to see a policeman escorting Dallas to his car. She hoped Dallas would push the cop and get arrested. She quickly fantasized about Dallas being taken to jail on a Saturday night, where he'd surely be beaten by other inmates in the cell that didn't like men in tuxes. The jailers wouldn't interfere because Dallas was arrested for resisting arrest by one of their fellow officers.

Helen snapped out of her fantasy when one of Larry's golf buddies approached and gave her a drunken hug and a kiss. Larry started talking about his golf game and Helen slipped away through the crowd. She walked up to the bar next to the Banyan tree and ordered a Chardonnay. As she took a sip, Bryce walked up from behind her and said, "Good evening, gorgeous."

Helen turned and looked at Bryce dressed impeccably in his Armani tuxedo with a purple cummerbund. Her body remembered how passionate their last nooner had been, but her head overruled and she asked icily, "Why should I even talk to you?"

He patted his cummerbund. "Because we match tonight; it's destiny."

Helen turned and walked away as she said, "Get a life." She walked about ten steps and turned to look back at Bryce. He was looking at her butt and smiling. She secretly was happy Bryce was looking, but she quickly walked back
148

to her husband and joined the boring conversation. After five minutes of boasting, the group moved to the bar and stayed there for the next hour. Helen drank three glasses of Chardonnay and watched everyone arriving for the gala. She checked for good-looking men and confirmed that no other woman had a gown similar to hers.

Helen was disappointed that she'd seen no men that interested her. Except for Bryce. She told her husband she was going to the bathroom and walked through the crowd. McGregor Boulevard divided the estate, and normally a crosswalk with a traffic light allowed foot traffic between each side. During the annual fundraiser, the road was blocked off and traffic detoured around the estate. A portable stage was set up on the closed-off portion of the road, and a band entertained the crowd with jazz standards. Some couples were dancing to the high-energy band on the roadway and others sat at tables and caught up with the latest gossip. The palm trees that lined McGregor Boulevard lit up with strings of small white lights, circling their trunks and extending twenty-five feet into the air.

Helen watched everyone having fun and suddenly felt very lonely. She walked over to another bar set up next to the palm trees on the river side of the estate. She got another Chardonnay and strolled over to Mina Edison's moonlight garden to smell the night-blooming jasmine. It was dimly lit and no one else was nearby, so she sat down on a cement bench looking over the ten-foot long shallow pool, filled with water lilies. She looked back towards the band, belting out old favorites. A few minutes later, she heard some footsteps behind her and turned around to see Bryce.

He said, "I've been looking for you."

Helen stood up and faced Bryce as she said quietly, "If

my husband sees us talking, he'll kill you."

Bryce stepped toward Helen and lowered his voice, "I'll take my chances. I can't deny it any longer—I love you."

Helen was shocked. "You're just saying that because you want to fool around."

Bryce pleaded. "No, I mean it."

Bryce put his arms around Helen's waist and pulled her to him. Helen's mind told her to leave, but the wine and her body voted for a kiss. The kiss quickly became passionate, and they pulled close. After a minute, Helen pulled back and said, "I've got to go. He'll miss me."

Bryce frowned and reluctantly said, "Okay."

Helen ran her hands through her hair and sighed. Bryce looked at his watch and said quietly. "I've got an idea. Go back to Larry and keep him entertained with his buddies for a while. Meet me at midnight at the garage behind the garden. We can have some fun in that old model T Ford."

Helen hesitated. "I don't know."

Bryce pleaded. "Please. I've missed you."

Helen weighed the pros and cons for a few seconds and whispered, "Okay, I'll see you at midnight. Wait here for a few minutes until I get back to the bar."

Bryce smiled and nodded slowly. Helen turned and walked back toward the band and her husband. As she walked toward the bright lights of the stage and seating area, she thought about the upcoming midnight tryst. Bryce had been intimate with her hundreds of times and never said he loved her. She needed his financial help a few months before and he avoided her. Now Bryce wanted her for a quirky fantasy. The more she compared his actions to those magical words, the more confused she got.

As she got closer to the band and the tables covered

with white tablecloths, she saw two of her girlfriends waving her over to their table. Helen walked over to the two bleach blonde women with empty wine glasses and said, "Hello, Kathy. You look great tonight."

A tall blonde stood up and gave Helen a cheek kiss as she said, "You look exquisite. Where did you get that dress?"

Helen answered proudly, "Down at Naples on Fifth Avenue. Where'd you get yours?"

Kathy answered, "At Saks. But Linda here flew to New York City for her dress; didn't you, honey?"

As everyone sat down Linda gushed, "My husband flew us up for our tenth anniversary. It was fun."

A waitress walked up with a tray of glasses filled with wine. They all grabbed a glass and took a sip. Helen looked at Kathy and asked, "So who's your date tonight?" Kathy sighed, "I'm here with Dave, my old faithful."

The women looked toward the band and smiled as an elderly couple danced cheek to cheek, awkwardly moving with the slow music. They all took a drink of their wine and silently wondered if they would have someone to dance with at that age.

Kathy put her glass down and looked sympathetically at Helen. "Oh, by the way, I'm sorry things didn't work out for you with Dallas's real estate firm."

Helen's face flushed. "How'd you hear about that?"

Kathy pointed toward the giant banyan tree. "When we first got here tonight, Dallas came up and started talking to us. He told us you quit because you weren't bringing in new listings and the pressure of working on commission got to you. He told us he thought you were discouraged when you failed the real estate exam."

Helen ground her teeth. "Is that what he told you?"

151

Kathy nodded and raiser her eyebrows. "Was there something else?"

Helen started to tell Kathy exactly what happened, but she looked over at Linda and saw her listening intently Then it hit her—it was all a setup. They were trying to get the lowdown on her firing and start some gossip. Helen took a deep breath before she answered through clenched teeth, "No, that's pretty much what happened."

They all smiled politely and took a drink of their wine. Helen set her glass down and stood up. "I'm going back to find my husband. Have a nice night."

As Helen walked away, her head was swirling with anger. Her supposed friends were trying to dig up dirt on why Dallas was going around town trashing her. She was sick of Dallas and his lies. It was bad enough he stole from her— now he was ruining her reputation.

As Helen approached the bar, she saw her husband leaning on the bar and talking to the same golf buddies. She walked up behind Larry and put her hand on his back, "Hi, honey."

Larry turned around and put his arm around her. "I wondered where you went."

Helen squeezed Larry close and whispered, "I didn't want to bother you, so I went down and listened to the band with some of my girlfriends."

One of the golfing buddies slurred, "Larry, tell us about that birdie out of the sand trap at Hilton Head last year."

Larry straightened up, "Oh, you don't want to hear about that one again, do you?"
His buddies started chanting, "Larry. Larry. Larry."

Larry looked back at Helen and she smiled, nodding toward his buddies, "Go ahead and have some fun. I'm going to the bathroom."

Helen walked to the end of the bar and ordered tw
tequila shots, hoping they would help her headache. She
downed them back to back and her headache intensified.
She walked through the dimly lit main parking lot, toward
her Suburban parked in the rear lot to get some aspirin.
Helen was thinking of how she could get back at Dallas,
when she saw Bryce kissing and fondling a young blonde,
leaning against his Porsche parked next to a giant oak tree.
She ducked into the shadows and watched Bryce and the
young woman kiss and grope each other. After a few
minutes, they climbed into his Porsche and quickly fogged
up the windows.

Helen couldn't contain herself, and she snuck up
behind the Porsche, intent on creating a scene. As she
approached the left rear of the car, she heard the young
woman say, "Who was that redhead in the purple dress I
saw you talking to?"

Bryce didn't miss a beat. "She's nothing."

Helen heard the woman giggling as her blood boiled
with betrayal. She imagined the instant gratification a
confrontation would cause, but decided to wait and
formulate a plan. She walked to the edge of the parking lot
so Bryce couldn't see her and took the long way. As she
walked oward her Suburban, her hands were shaking with
rage. She realized that she was nothing but a conquest for
Bryce; a double-header played at the Edison Home. She
thought about the handgun in her purse and shooting Bryce
in his beloved Porsche, but then she remembered the
midnight rendezvous. She'd told Bryce she'd meet him at
midnight, and by God, she'd meet him. She looked at her
watch and saw she had thirty minutes to formulate a plan.

A year before one of Helen's friends was mugged in the parking lot of a mall. Her friend convinced Helen to take a concealed weapon's class with her so they could carry small guns in their purses for protection. They went to Billy's Gun Range, and he sold both women a .22 caliber semi-automatic gun for their purses. It took them a week of shooting the gun and getting familiar with its operation before Billy let them take the concealed weapons class. Helen's friend was content to legally have the gun in her purse, but Helen liked shooting hers. Helen came back to the range every day for a month without her friend.

During this time at the range, she became friends with Billy, a retired cop from Detroit. Billy told her stories of his days on the force and how there'd be less crime if everyone carried a gun. He loved telling stories of criminals getting shot when they tried to attack someone carrying a hidden gun. Helen couldn't forget the near abduction of her daughters and how Ray got lucky wrestling the gun from the stranger. Helen soaked it all up and was determined to be a good shot.

Billy explained to her that you should always shoot to kill, because criminals would make up stories about how they were the victim, and some of their dishonest friends could provide corroborating witness statements to the cops. All the street-wise criminals called this "flip the script." He told her a story of how one of his buddies got in trouble over a shooting when he was attacked coming from a high-stakes poker game with a bunch of cash. He left an apartment complex at three in the morning and two guys were waiting in the shadows for him. When they approached, he pulled his gun and shot one in the thigh, while holding his gun on the other.

Neighbors heard the shots and called 911. The cops investigated, and the two men said they were just asking for directions. Billy's friend was convicted of aggravated battery with a firearm and served ten years in prison. Billy explained to Helen that if you carry a gun, you should file off the serial number so it can't be traced to you if you shoot someone that needs shooting, but you don't want to risk any problems with the cops. Kill the bad guy, wipe your fingerprints and ditch the gun. The good guys win.

Helen was intrigued with vigilante justice and asked Billy if she needed to know anything else. Billy smiled and nodded his head. He loved showing off his knowledge to the pretty redhead. He told her a lot of shooters were caught because of fingerprints on the bullet casings. When Helen asked him to explain, he pulled his 9mm Glock from his holster and popped out the clip. He emptied the bullets and laid them on the table. As he picked up the bullets and reloaded the clip, he explained how the smooth surface on the bullet casings held fingerprints for a long time. When a bullet was fired, a casing was ejected from the gun and landed on the ground near where it was shot. The fingerprint on the casing is what a lot of criminals forgot about and tied them to a shooting. He explained the bullets should be loaded in the clip while wearing gloves.

Billy counseled Helen that if she was going to carry a gun she needed to be prepared. Billy explained if you had to shoot a bad guy in an embarrassing place, you could wipe your fingerprints from your gun with no serial number, throw the gun away, and not worry about fingerprints on the casings. Billy explained how to best kill a person and everything police looked for in the crime scene investigation.

Helen decided to follow her mentor's advice and asked Billy to help her file the serial number off her gun. Billy took her to the maintenance room of the firing range and put her gun in a vise. He used his handheld grinder and filed off the number. Helen was ready for any bad guy that might attack.

** ** ** ** **

Helen thought of a plan as she walked to her Suburban. She opened the rear cargo area and grabbed a fifteen-foot blue boater's rope, a yellow bungee cord, and two old rags. She stuffed them into her purse and headed back to her husband and his buddies. She walked the long way back so she wouldn't see Bryce's fogged up Porsche.

As Helen approached the bar, she saw her husband still drinking with his golfing buddies. She'd volunteered to be the designated driver so he could get sloshed with his friends. She'd had her fair share to drink, but her adrenaline had sobered her up. She came up behind him and pinched his butt. He jumped forward and turned as he said, "That'll get your attention."

Helen gave him a big hug and looked over at his buddies. "You boys don't get my man too drunk. He's gonna need his energy later."
Larry looked surprised. "Really?"

Helen smiled. "Oh, yeah. I'm gonna go see my girlfriends for a little while and then I'll be back."

Helen smiled and gave her husband a kiss on the lips. As she was walking away, she heard one of Larry's buddies offering him a blue pill. Helen walked past the band on McGregor Boulevard and back to Mina Edison's moonlight garden. She sat down on the cement bench next to the nightblooming jasmine, facing the garage with the 1919 Model T, and went over her plan again. There was bougainvillea on the other side of the garden that partially blocked her view of the garage, but she saw some light in the garage, through the branches.

At 11:59 p.m. she started walking over to the garage. Most of the people that were left at the fundraiser had gathered around the bars or the band. As she left the shadows of the garden, she saw the lights go off in the garage. It took her about fifteen seconds to walk up to the garage and open the old fashioned side swinging garage doors. She saw Bryce leaning on the Model T Ford, and she smiled. She turned and looked behind her to make sure there were no witnesses and quietly closed the swinging doors. She turned toward Bryce and ran her hands through her hair.

Bryce said quietly, "I wondered if you were coming."

Helen smiled. "I always keep my word. Hurry up; I can only be away for a few minutes."

Bryce walked over to Helen and gave her a quick kiss. He walked over and locked the garage door. There was one foot square glass panels on the top of the garage doors that let in some light from the waning moon. Helen and Bryce embraced and kissed passionately as they listened to the band loudly playing crowd favorites.

After about ten seconds Helen broke off the kiss and said, "Strip down and get in the driver's seat. I brought some rope so we can do it the way you like it."

Bryce's eyes lit up with excitement. "Really!"

Helen whispered, "Oh, yeah."

Bryce took off his clothes so fast he almost tripped over his black silk boxers when his feet got tangled. Helen got into the passenger seat as Bryce got situated in the driver's seat. Helen opened her purse and took out the rope and the bungee cord. She wrapped the rope around Bryce and the seat and pulled the end of the rope through the loop on the opposite end.

She pulled the rope tight around Bryce and tied a knot. She kissed his right ear and whispered, "Put your hands up on the wheel."

Bryce gladly complied.

Helen grabbed the yellow bungee cord and secured Bryce's hands tightly to the wheel. She leaned into Bryce and ran her hand over his chest and kissed his neck. She whispered, "I want you to close your eyes and remember that night on the beach by the Sanibel Lighthouse."

Bryce quietly groaned with pleasure. "Touch me."

Helen leaned forward in her seat and picked up her purse from the floor board as she said, "Oh honey, I will in a second. Just think about the beach."

Bryce closed his eyes and groaned again as Helen rubbed her hands down his thigh, and reached for the gun out of her purse with her right hand, listening for anyone near the garage. She listened for three seconds and then pushed the gun into Bryce's skin over his heart.

The last words Bryce ever said were, "Oh, baby."

Helen pushed harder into Bryce's chest so it would act as a silencer and squeezed the trigger twice. Bryce's body twitched and his head slumped over to Helen's side. Helen looked at Bryce's wide open eyes and said, "You wanted a double header, but you got a double tap."

Helen's heart was pounding, but she forced herself to follow her plan. She pulled the rags out of her purse and wrapped one around the gun, putting it back in her purse. She used the other to wipe her fingerprints off the seat and
158

wheel. She got out of the Model T and wiped down the outside handle. She walked to the garage door, unlocked it, and grabbed the handle with the rag. She wiped the handle clean and slowly cracked it open, peeking both ways and seeing no one. She closed the door with the rag, wiped it clean, and stuffed the rag into her purse. She walked the opposite way in the shadows. Once she was back to McGregor Boulevard, she came out of the shadows and carefully walked to the bar, as if she didn't have a care in the world on this lovely evening.

Helen walked up behind her husband and wrapped her hands around his waist, "Hey honey, let's get out of here."

Larry turned around and pulled Helen close. "I wondered when you were coming back."

Helen looked at Larry's buddies and winked. "We gotta go. He's got to make his wife happy tonight."

All of Larry's buddies looked at him enviously as he clumsily waved goodbye and walked toward the parking lot with his arm around Helen. Helen flirted and laughed with Larry all the way home. Once they got home, she steered her drunk husband to his bedroom and stripped him down. She pushed him onto the bed and stripped down herself. She thought of Brad Pitt as she had nuisance sex with her husband. He finished quickly and was sleeping within five minutes, just as she planned.

Helen grabbed her clothes and purse and walked back to her bedroom. She showered and dressed in black jeans with a black T-shirt. She walked to her Suburban and put her purse in the rear cargo area. It was two in the morning by the time she got to Dallas's house. She drove around the block to make sure no one was out walking a dog in the neighborhood. After she was satisfied with the lack of witnesses, she parked in front of Dallas's house.

She got her purse and walked up Dallas's driveway to his BMW. She used the second rag to open the car door with her right hand and set her purse on the driver's seat. She took out the rag wrapped around the gun with her left hand. While holding the gun with the rag, she used the second rag with her right hand to wipe her fingerprints from the gun. With her left hand in the rag, she slid the gun under the driver's seat, put the rag in her purse, and quietly shut the door with her right hand and the second rag. She put the second rag in her purse and looked around to confirm no witnesses.

Helen looked up toward Dallas's house and quietly said, "Nice doing business with you."

Chapter 15

Thursday 1:05 p.m.

"The State calls Leonard Fletcher."

The assistant bailiff opened the witness room and called his name. An elderly gentleman dressed in a faded blue pinstriped suit and red tie walked out of the witness room and shuffled over to the clerk, who swore him in. The head bailiff helped him up the steps to the witness stand. Spere said, "Please give us your name and address." Fletcher adjusted his eyeglasses and focused on Spere. "You know my name. I was in your office just a little while ago."

There were a few snickers in the courtroom, and Spere said in quieter voice, "Mr. Fletcher, I know your name, but one of the rules of court is you have to let the jury know your name before you testify. Could you please tell the jury your name?"

Fletcher looked over at the jury. "My name is Leonard Fletcher. Nice to meet you people."

Two female jurors giggled quietly. Spere asked, "Sir, do you remember the big party at the Edison Home back on January eighteenth of this year?"

"Sure do. My dentures fell out when I bit into one of those stale meatballs."

More people giggled. Spere realized he had to ask very specific questions, or this witness was going to have the jurors laughing. Spere liked somber jurors that were angry at the defendant; laughing jurors were more likely to acquit.

Spere spoke in a more authoritative tone, "Mr. Leonard, do you remember that Bryce Cervante was murdered at the Edison Home that night?"

Fletcher nodded. "That's what that mullet wrapper of a newspaper said."

Judge Stalman was laughing along with everyone else in the courtroom. Spere was not happy with Mr. Fletcher's antics, so he decided to focus on the defendant and asked, "Do you see Dallas Kelley here in the courtroom?"

Fletcher looked over at the defense table and pointed, "Yeah, that's him next to his shyster lawyer."

The laughter was louder, and Spere was grinding his teeth he was so mad. Ray started to object, but thought better of it. He stood up, and shrugged his shoulders as he said in a cheerful voice, "Judge, we'll stipulate he identified Mr. Kelley."

Everyone in the courtroom was cracking up except for Spere. Not only had Fletcher made the jurors laugh, but the defense lawyer had joined the party. Spere waited until the laughter died down and asked, "Did you see Mr. Kelley and the victim fighting at the party?"

Fletcher nodded his head emphatically. "Sure did. They were by the bar, calling each other all sorts of names and talking about each other's mothers."

Judge Stalman bit his lower lip and put his hand in front of his mouth as courtroom laughter bounced off the walls. Spere raised his voice, "Did you ever hear any threats?"

"Yep," Fletcher nodded. "Dallas told Bryce he wasn't going to let him get away with stealing from him. He said he was gonna get him back. And then they talked about each other's mothers a little bit more."

All of the jurors were laughing. Spere whimpered, "No

further questions."

Ray stood up and walked to the podium. "Mr. Fletcher, if Bryce Cervante had stolen from my client, then what he said was truthful, isn't it?"

Fletcher sat back in his chair and scratched his chin for a few seconds. "I guess so. Like my granddaddy always used to say, 'If a frog had wings, he wouldn't bump his ass every time he jumped.'"

Everyone laughed. Ray was embarrassed, but he liked laughing jurors. "No further questions, Your Honor."

Judge Stalman waited until the laughter was finished. "Call your next witness."

Fletcher hadn't moved from the witness stand. He looked over at Judge Stalman and asked, "Do I have to go? I like it here."

Judge Stalman pointed to the main courtroom door. "Your time is up, sir. We need to finish this trial."

Fletcher got up and hobbled out of the courtroom as everyone laughed to themselves.
Spere announced, "The State calls Laverne Bent."

The assistant bailiff opened the witness room and called her name. A matronly lady in her late forties walked through the door. She was dressed in an expensive black dress, and her bottle red hair was perfectly coifed, with a part down the middle. Her makeup would've made Mary Kay beam with pride, and her jewelry would've made a jeweler jealous.

When the clerk asked her if she swore to tell the truth, she announced in a southern drawl, "I most certainly will."

After she sat down and looked up, Spere asked, "Could you give us your name and what you do for a living, please?"

She announced proudly, "My name is Laverne Bent,

163

and I'm a domestic engineer for my husband and three boys."

"Were you at the Edison Home on the night Bryce Cervante was killed?"

"Yes, I was."

"Could you tell the jury if you witnessed an argument between Bryce Cervante and Dallas Kelley?"

"Yes, I did. Bryce and I used to go to First Methodist, and we were talkin' about church business, when Mr. Kelley came up and grabbed his arm, and spun him around. I couldn't believe the language Mr. Kelley was usin'. He was accusin' Bryce of stealing from him. Fortunately, a couple of the men pulled 'em apart and stood between 'em until the police came."

"How angry did Mr. Kelley appear to you?"

Mrs. Bent sat back in her chair and took a deep breath. She had practiced her testimony in front of her bathroom mirror for months—it was finally show time. She looked at the jury and lowered her voice. "I've never seen a man as mad as Dallas Kelley. There was fire in his eyes, and his hands were shakin'. When he spoke, it was almost like a demon's voice. I felt a cold chill whenever he shouted out at poor Bryce."

After three seconds of silence Spere spoke in a solemn voice, "No further questions."

Judge Stalman asked, "Cross-examination?"

Ray stood up and walked to the podium. "What does a demon's voice sound like?"

Ms. Bent stammered, "Well, you know, kind of loud and evil sounding."

Ray rolled his eyes and asked, "Where exactly did you feel a cold chill when he shouted at poor Bryce?"

Ms. Bent had recovered. "It started in my neck and
164

went half-way down my back."

Ray pointed at Spere. "You know the prosecutor, Mr. Spere, don't you?"

"Why, yes. My youngest son plays little league baseball with his son."

"Did you meet with him to discuss your testimony?"
"We met yesterday at his office, in the afternoon."

Ray pointed again at Spere. "Mr. Spere was at the party at the Edison Home that night, wasn't he?"

"Yes, he was. There were a lot of people at the fund raiser. It's a very worthwhile cause and a lot of fun."
"Isn't it true, Mr. Spere was there with his wife?"

Ray saw Spere pushing his chair back, ready to spring forward with an objection. It was working exactly as he planned.

Mrs. Bent answered slowly, "Yes, she was there."
"Was she with Mr. Spere the entire time?"

Spere sprang up like a jack-in-the-box and yelled, "Objection, relevance."

Judge Stalman glared at Ray and growled, "Sidebar, counselor."

Ray and Spere walked up to the sidebar and waited for the court reporter to position herself between them. Ray decided to kill two birds with one stone: He was still angry at Spere for the comment he'd made to Amber the night before in the Veranda and he wanted to throw off Spere's timing.

Judge Stalman looked at Ray and hissed, "How is this line of questioning relevant?"

Ray took a deep breath before answering. "Judge, Mr. Spere always has black eyes, so it's a reasonable inference that his wife beats him up at home. If she is a violent person, it's a reasonable inference that she might've committed the murder. It's obvious from the evidence that the victim was having a romantic encounter when he was murdered. Maybe the prosecutor's wife killed him during a romantic encounter. Or maybe the prosecutor walked up on a tryst between his wife and the victim and he killed him out of jealousy."

Spere's eyes were bulging and the veins in his forehead were visibly pulsing as he blurted out, "That's ridiculous. Judge, I want you to hold him in contempt."

Judge Stalman glared at Ray and asked sternly, "Do you have any evidence to support your wild allegations?"

Ray hesitated. "I've seen Mr. Spere with a lot of black eyes, Your Honor."

Judge Stalman whispered through clenched teeth, "I was there with my wife; maybe she killed him? By the way, your wife was there too."

Ray responded quickly, "Ex-wife."

Judge Stalman realized he'd hit a nerve. "Your wife has quite the reputation. If I let you ask about Spere's wife, I'll let Spere ask about your wife."

Ray whispered, "Ex-wife."

Judge Stalman raised his voice, "Move along, counselor."

The lawyers and court reporter returned to their positions. Ray looked up at Judge Stalman and announced, "No further questions."

Spere stood up and said in a bitter voice, "The State rests."

Judge Stalman boomed, "Does the defense wish to put on a case?"

Ray answered, "Yes, Your Honor. I have four witnesses in the witness room."

Judge Stalman growled. "Call you first witness."

Ray looked over at the assistant bailiff standing by the defense witness room. "The Defense calls Doug Shearer."

The assistant bailiff opened the witness room and called his name. Doug walked to the door and shook hands with the bailiff, an old friend, and then walked confidently toward the clerk. After he was sworn in, he stepped up to the witness stand and sat down. He pulled the microphone toward him and looked up at Ray.

"Please tell the jury your name." "My name is Doug Shearer."

"Where did you go to college?"

"I went to Florida State University on a football scholarship, and I received my degree in criminology."

"Where did you start working after college?"

"I worked at the Lee County Sheriff's Office. I started out as a road deputy and worked my way up to detective."

"How long did you work at the sheriff's department?"

"Seventeen years."

"Why did you leave the sheriff's department?"

"I was fed up with the bureaucracy and tunnel-vision of my supervisors."

Ray looked over at Spere and then the jury before continuing. "What work did you start doing after you left the department?"

"I started my own investigation firm."

"Did I hire you to assist me in the defense of Dallas Kelley?"

Doug nodded. "Yes, you did."

"During your investigation, did you find three different women that the victim, Bryce Cervante, was dating?"

"Yes, I did."

"How did you find out this information?"

"You got a court order to allow us to search the

victim's home and office for any material that might help the defense. We copied his Rolodex and daily planner and looked for matches. We cross-referenced his cell phone records with his home and office phone records and then matched those numbers to names in his little black book he kept in his nightstand, next to his bed."

There were a few muffled laughs in the court that were quickly silenced when Judge Stalman looked up.

Ray continued, "Who were these three women?"

"Karen Gilmore, Shirley North, and Tammy Rothchild."

"Did you interview each of these women separately?" "I did, and before the interviews, I swore each of them

"Did you explain to them if they lied under oath they could be sentenced to five years in prison?" "Yes, I did."

"Were they reluctant to talk about their relationship to the victim?"

"No one likes talking about their dirty laundry, but I told them if they didn't cooperate, we could have a public hearing in front of a judge and courtroom full of newspaper reporters listening to all of the lurid details. I told them we were investigating a murder case, and it was important. After they thought about it, they cooperated and answered my questions under oath."

Ray hesitated and stepped to the side of the podium. "Mr. Shearer, are all of these women in the defense witness room at this time, pursuant to subpoenas you served on them?"

"Yes, they are."

Ray considered asking a question about if they were happy to be in court, but decided against it. He hesitated, and let the jury think about it.

"No further questions."

Judge Stalman looked over at Spere, who stood up and

walked to the podium. He sneered. "How much money have you been paid for your testimony?"

Doug looked Spere squarely in the eyes. "I haven't been paid for my testimony. I've been paid for my time."

Spere was speechless and looked angrily at Ray. Ray thought to himself *I can coach my witnesses too, asshole.*

Spere cleared his throat and asked in a saccharine voice, "How much money have you been paid for your time?"

Doug answered, "I charge seventy-five dollars per hour, and I have put in a little over 100 hours on the case before today. So, to answer your question, I have been paid $7,500 for my time."

Spere looked over at the jury and shook his head as he said, "No further questions."

As Doug stepped off the witness stand, Judge Stalman said, "Call your second witness."

Ray looked toward the assistant bailiff standing by the defense witness room and announced, "The Defense calls Karen Gilmore."

The assistant bailiff opened up the door and called out her name. A young blonde with a gymnast's body walked out of the doorway and looked toward Judge Stalman, who quickly sucked in his belly and sat up in his chair. Judge Stalman remembered his mentor's mantra: *Justice may be blind, but judges aren't.*

Judge Stalman motioned with his right hand toward the clerk as he said, "Please approach the clerk and be sworn in to tell the truth."

The clerk stood up and said, "Raise your right hand. Do you swear or affirm to tell the truth?"

Karen was dressed in a tight red dress with a plunging neckline that showed off her perky cleavage. She kept her hands to her side as she looked up at Judge Stalman and said in her best little girl voice, "I don't want to talk about Bryce, but the lawyer said you'd put me in jail if I don't. Is that true?"

Judge Stalman considered the request from this beautiful young woman and answered in a stern voice. "The Defense has the right to subpoena any witness that will help them.

So yes, you have to tell the truth and answer his questions," Judge Stalman looked over menacingly toward Ray. "Any relevant questions, that is."

Karen looked dejected her appeal didn't work, but raised her right hand reluctantly. "I swear to tell the truth."

Judge Stalman said in his sweetest voice, "Please walk over to the witness stand and have a seat."

Judge Stalman watched her every move as she maneuvered the witness chair into a comfortable position. He waited until she was situated and then slightly moved his chair to get the best available view of her cleavage. Ray said, "Please give us your name and age."

Karen answered, "My name is Karen Gilmore, and I'm eighteen."

"Do you attend college?"

"Yes, I'm a freshman at Florida Gulf Coast University."

"How did you know Bryce Cervante?"

"Bryce and my father were friends at the country club. I've known him since I was a kid."

"As you grew older, did you and Bryce become closer friends?"

Karen hesitated and shifted in her chair before answering. "Well, you know, I was a swimmer, and Bryce was a swimmer, so we'd swim laps at the same time at the
170

country club. And you know, as I got older, I talked to him more and more."

Ray hesitated and looked up at Judge Stalman who was glaring at him. "Did you ever flirt with Bryce while swimming together?"

Karen shifted in her chair. "Well, you know, he was always commenting about me, you know, filling out, so after a while, you know, I kinda flirted with him a little bit, I guess."

Ray nodded. "How did Bryce respond to this flirting?"

Karen smiled mischievously and said, "He called me jailbait. He told me to come see him when I turned eighteen."

Judge Stalman boomed, "Counselor, approach sidebar. Now."

Ray and Spere approached the sidebar, and Judge Stalman whispered loudly, "Where is this going, counselor?"

Ray answered, "Judge, I have a sworn statement from this witness that she was with the victim the night he died and had a sexual encounter in the parking lot of the Edison Home, and it ended badly."

Judge Stalman answered quietly, "Oh, I see. You may continue."

Ray returned to the podium and faced Karen. "Did you go see Bryce Cervante when you turned eighteen?"

Karen turned to Judge Stalman, "Do I have to answer this?"

Judge Stalman answered firmly, "Yes, you do."

Ray repeated, "Did you go see Bryce Cervante when you turned eighteen?"

Karen lowered her voice. "Yes." "What happened?"

"I went to his office after I got out of school and told

171

him I turned eighteen, and I was no longer jailbait. He asked for my driver's license and made a copy of it. And then we left his office and…"

Ray asked, "Did you go to his house?" "Yes."

"What happened next?"

Karen whispered, "We made love."

There was rumbling in the courtroom, but for once Judge Stalman waited a few seconds before he demanded order in the court.

After the courtroom quieted down, Ray asked, "This occurred about three months before Mr. Cervante was killed, correct?"

"Yes."

"Isn't it true you were lovers from your eighteenth birthday until the day Bryce Cervante died?"
Karen whispered, "Yes."

"Let's talk about the night Bryce died. Did you have a sexual encounter with Bryce that night?"

Karen looked down and whispered, "Yes." "Were you his date to the fundraiser?"

Karen took a deep breath. "No, I came to the fundraiser with my boyfriend."

There were more rumbles in the courtroom, and Judge Stalman said nothing as he looked at Karen in wonderment. He let the murmurs die a slow death and watched Karen squirming in her chair, looking down at her feet. Judge Stalman was enjoying watching this angelic beauty get her wings clipped in his courtroom. In fact, he was so excited he decided his wife was going to get the benefit of his full attention that night.

When it was quiet Ray continued. "How did you end up with Bryce Cervante?"
Karen pulled her hair out of her eyes and sat up. "Well I

was mad my boyfriend was ignoring me and was with his buddies at the bar talking about football, so I walked over to Bryce and asked if he wanted to go to his car. He said yes, so we went to the back of the parking lot and got in his Porsche."

"Isn't it true, you performed oral sex on Bryce Cervante in his Porsche?"

Karen hesitated and looked down as she answered quietly, "Yes."

"How did this encounter end?"

Karen took a deep breath and answered in a quivering voice, "Well, afterwards, I was resting my head on his shoulder and he said, 'Shirley, you're the best.'"

Ray shrugged his shoulders and raised his voice, "How did you react?"

Karen raised her voice, "I was mad as hell. I slapped him and got out of the car and slammed the door. I went back to my boyfriend at the bar."

"Isn't it true, after you slammed the door, you called Bryce Cervante an asshole?"

"Yes."

"Isn't it true, there were other people in the parking lot?" "Yes, I saw them as I was walking away."

"Isn't it true, these people in the parking lot told my investigator of your fight with Bryce the night he died?"

"I guess."

"My investigator contacted you a few days later and took your sworn statement about Bryce Cervante, didn't he?"

"Yes."

Ray hesitated to get the jurors full attention. "Didn't you tell him that Bryce Cervante liked oral sex better than regular sex?"

Spere stood up. "Objection."

Judge Stalman pointed at Ray and said firmly, "Sidebar."

After Ray and Spere got to the sidebar Judge Stalman asked, "How is this relevant?"

Ray explained, "Your Honor, it's relevant because the victim was found in a Model T Ford nude, with a smile on his face and no signs of a struggle. I want to show this witness had performed oral sex on the victim that night and became angry when she was called by the wrong name. She later decided to get revenge against the victim by luring him to the Model T with the promise of more oral sex and killed him out of anger."

Judge Stalman scratched his chin and considered the argument. After a few seconds, he smiled and said quietly, "The problem with that argument, counselor, is that the victim had already ejaculated, so he wouldn't have been able to do it again."

Ray smiled slyly and answered, "Your Honor, some men are one-hit-wonders, but other men are just getting started with one time."

Judge Stalman frowned and couldn't think how to respond on the record without an incriminating statement.

Ray continued, "Judge, I'll let Mr. Spere argue that he could only do it once, but I'll argue that Bryce Cervante just had his engine started, and he was ready to perform again."

Spere's face was turning bright red, but he said nothing.

Judge Stalman answered dourly, "You can ask your question."

Ray returned to the podium and looked at Karen. "Didn't you tell my investigator that Bryce Cervante liked
174

oral sex better than regular sex?"

Karen looked down and answered quietly, "Yes."

"Isn't it true, your boyfriend's family are members of the same country club where you and Bryce met?"

"Yes."

"Isn't it true, your boyfriend's mother is named Shirley?"

Karen's face flushed, and she glared at Ray for three seconds before she finally answered, "Yes."

There were more murmurs in the courtroom and Judge Stalman quickly ordered quiet in the court.

Ray announced, "No further questions."

Spere walked to the podium and asked, "Did you kill Bryce Cervante?"

Karen sat up straight in her chair and said loudly, "I did not."

"No further questions."

Judge Stalman looked at Karen. "You may step down." As Karen walked quickly out of the courtroom, Judge Stalman looked at Ray and said, "Next witness." "The defense calls Shirley North."

The assistant bailiff opened the defense witness room and called her out. A tall brunette, dressed in gray slacks, a white blouse, and a burgundy coat strode into court without hesitation and raised her right hand. The clerk swore her in and she sat down in the witness stand, glaring at Ray.

Ray asked, "Please give us your name and job title." "My name is Shirley North, and I run my own CPA firm."

"Are you married?" "I am divorced."

"Do you have any children?" "I have one son."

"Does he date Karen Gilmore?"

"Yes, they've dated since they were in high school."

Ray hesitated for few seconds and raised his voice, "Did you know Bryce Cervante?"

"Yes, I did."

"What was your relationship to him?" "We were friends."

Ray asked sarcastically, "Weren't you a little more than friends?"

Shirley sat back in her chair and glared at Ray for a few seconds before she answered. "We were both single, consenting adults. Sometimes, we dated."

Ray nodded. "Were you and Bryce members of the same country club?"

"Yes, we were."

"Did you ever notice that he was friendly with Karen Gilmore?"

Shirley shifted in her chair. "I noticed they seemed to be awfully chummy. It turns out my suspicions were right."

"That had to make you angry that your boyfriend was awfully chummy with your son's girlfriend."

Shirley attempted to dismiss Ray's innuendo. "Well, I didn't know at the time how chummy they were."

Ray looked at his notes for a second before he continued. "Did you attend the fundraiser at the Edison Home the night Bryce was murdered?"

Shirley nodded. "Yes, I did." "Did you have a date?"

"No, I went by myself. I knew there were going to be other single people there, so I went alone."

Ray hesitated a few seconds before he asked, "It had to make you angry that Bryce didn't invite you as his date?"

Ms. North sat up in her chair and raised her voice, "Bryce and I were adults. We could do as each of us pleased."

Ray raised his hands to his side and shrugged. "Well,
176

surely you hoped to dance with him at the fundraiser?"

"I hoped we would."

Ray raised his hands to his side. "But, you didn't?" Ms. North looked down and said quietly, "No." Ray raised his voice. "Isn't it true you had sex with Bryce Cervante the day before the fundraiser?"

Ms. North looked down and said quietly, "We were consenting adults."

"Is that a yes?"

Ms. North seethed. "Yes."

"You saw Bryce dancing with other women at the fundraiser, didn't you?"

"I don't remember."

Ray picked up her sworn statement that his investigator had taken two weeks after the murder and held it up with his left hand. "Do you remember a tape recorded interview with my investigator, Doug Shearer, about what happened that night? Would you like to review it?"

Ms. North took a deep breath. "Yes, I remember."

Ray shook the statement in the air. "Isn't it true that you saw Bryce dancing with other women that night?"

"I guess so. It's been so long."

Ray stepped to the side of the podium and held out the statement. "Would you like to review your statement to refresh your recollection?"

Ms. North shifted in her chair. "No, I don't need to review it. If I said it, I said it."

"Isn't it also true you saw Karen Gilmore walking to the parking lot with Bryce Cervante?"

"Yes, I saw them."

Ray hesitated to get the jurors' full attention. "How did you feel seeing your lover walking to the dark parking lot with your son's girlfriend after ignoring you all night?"

Spere sprang to his feet, "Objection."

Judge Stalman replied, "Overruled," and turned to Ms. North. "Answer the question."

Ms. North weighed her words before answering. "I was disappointed."

Ray looked over at the jury and raised his eyebrows. He then looked at Judge Stalman. "No further questions."

Spere walked to the podium. "Did you kill Bryce Cervante?"

Ms. North's face turned red and she looked over at the jury. "I didn't kill him, but I'm glad he's dead."

Spere shut his eyes and said quietly, "No further questions."

Judge Stalman dismissed Ms. North and looked over at Ray. "Any other witnesses?"

Ray looked over at the assistant bailiff and said loudly, "The Defense calls Tammy Rothchild."

The assistant bailiff opened the witness room and called her name. The witness room door opened, and a curly brown-haired woman walked in and looked around. She was dressed in a dark blue dress that was a size too small for her surgically-enhanced breasts. Judge Stalman motioned toward the clerk and she walked forward. When she raised her right hand to be sworn, Ray noticed she had long fake nails, painted bright red, and rings on every finger. After she was sworn in, she sat down in the witness stand and looked toward Ray.

Ray asked, "Please give us your name."

She answered in a heavy New York accent, "Tamara Sara Rothchild, but I go by Tammy."

"Mrs. Rothchild, are you married?" "Yes."

"How long have you been married?"

It'll be eighteen years next month."

"What does your husband do for a living?" "He's a diamond wholesaler."

"Does he travel a lot for his job?"

Mrs. Rothchild nodded. "Oh, yes. He travels back and forth between South Africa and Europe, making deals."

"Were you having an affair with Bryce Cervante before he died?"

Mrs. Rothchild shifted in her chair and took a deep breath. "My husband and I have an open marriage. He dates people, and so do I."

Ray used his best sarcastic voice. "So, were you and Bryce Cervante dating at the time he died?"

"Yes."

Ray held up some stapled papers. "Did my investigator take a sworn statement from you shortly after the murder of Bryce Cervante?"

Mrs. Rothchild looked at the papers. "Yes."

"Isn't it true, you had sex with Bryce Cervante the afternoon before the fundraiser?"

Mrs. Rothchild blushed. "Yes, we met at the Holiday Inn."

"Did you go to the fundraiser with your husband?" "Yes."

"Did you shower after your afternoon tryst with Bryce Cervante before you went home to your husband?"

Spere sprang to his feet. "Objection." Judge Stalman yelled, "Sustained."

Ray looked over at Mrs. Rothchild. She was beet red and glaring at Ray, which is what he'd wanted. He wanted her angry before his next line of questions.

Ray continued, "Isn't it true, you were angry that Bryce ignored you at the fundraiser?"

Mrs. Rothchild considered her answer. "I was a little

angry that he avoided my glances at the party. He was focusing his attention on some young blonde bimbo."

"Was this young blonde bimbo in the defense witness room with you earlier?" "Yes."

Ray raised his voice. "Do you have a concealed weapon permit?"

"I do."

"Do you own any hand guns?"

"Yes, I own a 9 mm Glock that I keep in my nightstand. I carry a .22 in my purse, and I keep a .38 in the glove compartment of my Mercedes."

Ray looked over at the jury and saw a few raised eyebrows. He hesitated and let the jury focus on her answer and draw their own conclusions.

"Isn't it true that the night of the murder you had a .22 in your purse?"

"Yes, I always do. My dad was a jeweler in New York City, and he raised us to carry guns for our protection. I've always carried a gun in my purse in case someone tries to steal my jewelry."

"If someone tried to steal your jewelry, what would you do?"

Mrs. Rothchild answered emphatically, "I'd shoot them."

Spere sprang to his feet. "Objection."

Judge Stalman scratched his chin, "Overruled."

Ray raised his voice. "If you'd shoot someone that tried to steal your jewelry, you'd shoot someone that had stole your heart and threw it away, wouldn't you?"

Spere sprang up. "Objection." "Sustained."

Ray hesitated for a few seconds and lowered his voice. "Did the police ever test your gun to see if it was the murder weapon?"

180

Spere sprang back up, "Objection, she's not on trial."

Judge Stalman looked over at Spere and shook his head, "Overruled. Sit down Mr. Spere."

Ray followed, "I ask you again, did the police ever test your gun to see if it was the murder weapon?"

"No, they did not. No one ever asked, but I'd be happy to let them test it."

"No further questions."

Spere stood up and asked loudly, "Did you kill Bryce Cervante?"

"I did not."

"No further questions."

Judge Stalman looked over at Mrs. Rothchild. "You may step down."

As she was leaving the courtroom, Judge Stalman looked over at Ray and asked, "Any other witnesses?"

Ray knew experienced trial attorneys would tell you the vast majority of the time a defendant should never testify. If a defendant doesn't testify then the jury focuses on whether or not the State's evidence proves the defendant guilty beyond all reasonable doubt. The defendant should only testify if he is believable and can add something to the case besides denying he did the crime. When the defendant testifies, the jury compares the defendant's story to the State's evidence, rather than focusing just on the State's evidence. Ray and Dallas had discussed the different strategies, and Ray advised him not to testify.

Dallas disagreed.

Chapter 16

Thursday afternoon, 2:24 p.m.

Ray stood up and announced, "The Defense calls Dallas Kelley."

Dallas walked in front of the defense table and raised his right hand as he looked at the clerk.

The clerk asked, "Do you swear or affirm to tell the truth, the whole truth, and nothing but the truth?" Dallas turned and looked at the jury. "I do."

Judge Stalman nodded toward the witness stand and said, "Sit in the witness chair."

Dallas walked quickly to the witness stand and got comfortable in the chair. He confidently pulled the microphone close and looked up at Ray.

Ray said, "Give us your name for the record." "My name is Dallas Eugene Kelley."

"Where were you born, Dallas?"

Dallas smiled. "I was born in Odessa, Texas."

There were a few chuckles in the courtroom. Ray continued, "How'd you get the name Dallas?"

Dallas scratched his chin. "My mom told me that she always wanted to move to the big city, but she figured she'd never leave, so she hoped the name would motivate me."

Ray shrugged and raised his hands in a questioning manner. "Where did you go to college?"

"The University of Houston."

More people laughed, including Judge Stalman. Spere was seething. He started to object out of anger, but realized he'd be overruled. He sat on his hands and silently cursed Ray for arranging his questions to get a laugh from the jury.

Ray continued, "What did you get your degree in?" "I majored in finance and got a minor in history." "How'd you end up in Ft. Myers?"

Dallas shifted in his chair and took a deep breath. "My college sweetheart was from here. We got engaged our senior year and moved back here after graduation and got married."

"What type of work did you do?"

"Her dad was a real estate broker at the beach. I started working for him, selling waterfront condos."

"How long did you work selling condos for your wife's father?"

Dallas's left eye twitched and he took a deep breath. "I worked for him for five years until my wife died during childbirth."

There was a collective gasp in the courtroom. Spere had heard enough. He stood up and roared, "Objection, Your Honor. How the defendant's wife died has absolutely no relevance to the case at hand."

Judge Stalman looked over at Ray. "What do you have to say, counselor?"

Ray answered, "Judge, the jury has the right to know the defendant's educational background and work background when evaluating his testimony. My next question will show the relevance."

Judge Stalman glared at Spere. "I agree. Sit down, Mr. Spere, your objection is overruled." He nodded toward Ray, "You may continue, Mr. Harrison."

Spere's fingers were shaking, he was so mad. Ray was successfully humanizing Dallas, and Spere didn't like it one bit. He couldn't wait for cross-examination.

Ray continued, "Why did you stop working for your wife's father?"

Dallas answered quietly, "It was very stressful for both of us being together. I think we reminded each other of her. We agreed amicably that I would start my own brokerage firm dealing with homes in town."

Ray stepped to the side of the podium and raised his voice, "Do you still have your own brokerage firm?"

Dallas nodded. "I still have my brokerage firm, but we have expanded into real estate development of gated communities. For the past ten years I have concentrated on building and selling homes in new developments in Ft. Myers and Naples."

Ray cleared his throat and asked solemnly, "How did you know Bryce Cervante?"

Dallas coughed and collected his thoughts before answering. "He'd been my lawyer for the past ten years. He handled any permitting or zoning issues for my company. He always did a good job for me until last year."

"Did you become angry with him last year?"

Dallas sat up and leaned forward, raising his voice, "Yes, I did. I paid him a lot of money to get my development through the permitting stage. I found out at the final hearing he used an expert witness for one of his other clients to trash my development. I then found out a few weeks later at a golf course that he was an investor in the other development. He sacrificed my development for one he was an investor in; he stole from me."

"Did you talk to Mr. Cervante the night he was killed?"

"Yes, I did. I confronted him at the fundraiser at the Edison Home. A lot of his clients were there, and I figured it was the best way to get back at him. There's nothing worse than embarrassing a lawyer in front of his clients."

Ray pointed his finger at Dallas and asked forcefully, "Did you kill Bryce Cervante?"

Dallas sat up straight in his chair and announced indignantly, "I did not."

Ray looked up at the judge. "No other questions."

Judge Stalman looked over at Spere. "Cross?"

Spere stood up and slid his chair backwards. "Yes, Your Honor. I have a number of questions for the defendant."

Spere walked calmly up to the podium and set down his notes. He looked up and stared at Dallas for a few seconds before he asked, "How much money did Bryce Cervante steal from you?"

Dallas seethed. "Five hundred thousand dollars."

A few of the jurors looked at each other with raised eyebrows. Spere waited a couple of seconds to let the jury digest the motive for murder before he continued. "How did you feel when he stole five hundred thousand dollars from you?"

Dallas cracked his knuckles. "I was mad as hell."

Spere pointed at Dallas and raised his voice, "Isn't it true, you were mad enough to contact the local TV station and try to get the investigative reporter to do a story on Mr. Cervante?"

"Yes, that's true."

Spere continued to point at Dallas. "Isn't it true, you were mad enough to report Mr. Cervante to the Florida Bar for unethical conduct?"

Dallas answered proudly, "Yes, that's true."

Spere continued to point at Dallas. "Isn't it true, you were mad enough to break the windows at his law office with a golf club."

186

Dallas smiled. "Yes, it was a nine iron."

Spere crossed his arms. "Isn't it true that on the night he was murdered, you shoved him and threatened him?"

Dallas hesitated. He didn't like where this line of questioning was going, so he tried to slow it down. "I shoved him, but I didn't really threaten him. I was trying to embarrass him in front of his other clients."

Spere looked down at his notes. "Isn't it true, you yelled to the police officer that had removed you from the Edison Home property, 'Tell that cocksucker I'm not done with him'?"

Dallas lowered his voice. "I said it, but it wasn't a threat; I was mad."

Spere looked around the courtroom and settled on the jury as he was shaking his head. He asked quietly, "Isn't it true, you killed Bryce Cervante?"

Dallas sat up straight in his chair and yelled, "No, it's not!"

Spere shouted, "Is that answer just as truthful as your claim, 'Tell that cocksucker I'm not done with him' was not a threat?"

Ray jumped to feet. "Objection, argumentative."

"Sustained."

Spere was just getting started. He let the loud exchange echo around the courtroom for five seconds before asking, "Isn't it true, the real reason you left your father-in-law's brokerage firm is that he was angry at you for remarrying six months after his daughter died?"

Ray started to object, but he knew he'd be overruled because he opened the door. He looked at Dallas shifting in his seat, searching for words and realized he'd miscalculated Spere's knowledge of Dallas's background.

Dallas stammered, "We'd already agreed that I was

going to branch out and start my own firm. I remarried after I had already opened my own firm. It had nothing to do with my new wife."

Spere smiled as he walked over to his table and opened up his trial notebook. He pulled out three official looking documents and looked up a Judge Stalman. "May I approach the witness?"

Judge Stalman nodded. "You may."

Spere walked toward Dallas as he said, "I'm showing you State's Exhibit 67. It's a certified copy of your original occupational license for your brokerage firm. Do you recognize it?"

Spere handed the document to Dallas. He glanced over it and looked up as he said, "Yes, I recognize it. It's my license."

"Could you tell the jury the date the license was issued?" Dallas looked over the document for a few seconds, searching for the date. "It was issued on July twenty-first, nineteen ninety-four."

Spere handed him the second document as he said, "I'm showing you State's Exhibit 68. Do you recognize it?"

Dallas turned pale as he looked over the exhibit. He eventually answered, "It's my marriage license for my second wife."

Spere raised his voice, "Could you tell the jury the date on the license?"

Dallas looked down at the document and back at Spere. "July ninth, nineteen ninety-four."

The jurors looked at each other and shook their heads.

Judge Stalman looked at Ray, who looked over at Spere, who was smiling.

After three seconds of silence in the courtroom, Spere

188

tightened the noose. "Mr. Kelley, do you still expect the jury to believe you left your father-in-law's firm because you wanted to start your own firm?"

Dallas pleaded, "Yes, that's true. I didn't know I had to get my occupational license. I thought my accountant had done it when he set up all the legal papers with the IRS. When I was getting ready for my first closing, the title company told me I didn't have a license, so I went down and got one."

Spere smiled because the hole was getting deeper. "Isn't it true, you got married on the same day you got your marriage license?"

Dallas stammered, "Yes."

Spere had the trap set. "Why did you get married on the same day?"

Dallas answered, "We were in love and wanted to get married."

Spere picked up the third document and walked towards Dallas as he said, "I'm showing you State's Exhibit 69. Do you recognize it?"

Dallas looked over the document and turned a lighter shade of pale. He finally said quietly, "I do. It's my son's birth certificate."

"Could you tell the jury the date of your son's birth?"

Dallas looked over at Ray, who looked down. Dallas looked up at Judge Stalman and stammered, "How is this related to the murder case?"

Judge Stalman relished his power. He said firmly, "Answer the question."

Dallas looked at Spere. "February 9, 1995."

Spere scratched his head. "By my calculations, that means your wife was two months pregnant at the time you married." Spere let the significance register with the jury and continued in a louder voice. "So, you lied when you told the jury the reason you married on the same day you got your marriage certificate was because you were in love."

Dallas whispered, "We were in love."

Spere moved in for the kill. "I suppose the next thing you're gonna try to tell this jury is that your son was two months premature."

Ray stood up. "Objection. Argumentative."

Judge Stalman boomed. "Sustained."

Spere was beaming. He pointed at Dallas and asked angrily, "Mr. Kelley, does lying under oath come easy for you?"

Ray stood up. "Objection. Argumentative."

Judge Stalman boomed. "Sustained."

Spere looked at the jury. "No other questions."

Judge Stalman looked at Dallas. "Please return to your seat."

Dallas slowly got up and walked unsteadily back to his seat. Judge Stalman looked at Ray. "Any other witnesses?" Ray stood up. "The defense rests, Your Honor."

Judge Stalman looked over at the jury. "We're going to adjourn today. The attorneys and I are going to work on the jury instructions. You are dismissed until nine tomorrow morning."

Judge Stalman was raised in Atlanta by his preacher father and schoolteacher mother. He was their only child and was smothered with affection and expectations. Both of his parents demanded perfect grades and respectful behavior. He gave them both. Every morning he made his bed and flossed after every meal. His orderly rituals continued to his adult life and the way he ran his courtroom.

190

After the jury left the courtroom, Judge Stalman asked Spere, "Are there any additional instructions requested to what we have previously discussed by the State?"

Spere stood up. "Yes, Your Honor. I'm requesting the instruction on conflicting sworn testimony affecting a witness's credibility. The defendant has been caught in a number of lies. He claimed he left his father-in-law's employment because of them reminding each other of his first wife. We proved it was because of his new pregnant girlfriend.

"In addition, he claimed he got married because he was in love. We proved he actually got married because he had knocked up his girlfriend. Because of this proven false testimony under oath, we are requesting the conflicting sworn testimony instruction on witness credibility."

Ray stood up and roared, "Judge, this is an outrage. My client explained the reason for these apparent inconsistencies. They have not proven what he said was a lie. They can't prove what Dallas Kelley was thinking when he did something. The prosecutor is trying to use innuendo upon innuendo to claim my client lied on the stand. This is highly unethical and improper. I object to this instruction."

Judge Stalman was in all of his glory. All of the eyes in the courtroom were focused on him and he faked contemplation by running his hands through his hair, even though he already knew what he was going to do.

After five seconds he looked at Ray and said loudly, "Mr. Harrison, it amuses me you would accuse Mr. Spere of unethical conduct when you have pursued a defense theory that is questionable at best. I have allowed you wide latitude, and I intend to do the same for the State."

Judge Stalman looked at Spere and said, "I agree with

you, Mr. Spere. I am going to give the instruction, and the jury will have to decide what weight to give it in their deliberations."

Judge Stalman looked over at Ray, "Any additional instructions requested by the Defense?"

Ray ground his teeth for a second and then said dejectedly, "No, Your Honor."

Judge Stalman announced, "I will prepare the amended instructions and provide them to counsel tomorrow morning before closing arguments. We are adjourned for the day. I will see everyone tomorrow morning."

Chapter 17

Thursday evening, 5:24 p.m.

Ray walked out of the courthouse and felt the stifling humidity of a southwest Florida summer afternoon. While walking to the parking garage, he loosened his tie and took a deep breath as he considered the strong likelihood his client was innocent. It was a criminal defense lawyer's biggest nightmare—an innocent client who might well have convicted himself by testifying in his own defense. Ray could add his own addendum to the nightmare: the mother of his children was probably the real murderer.

But how? How could Helen have gone to the fundraiser with her husband, murdered Bryce, and planted the gun at Dallas's house? Ray didn't know the answer, but the jasmine perfume, bungee cord, and rope, coupled with Helen's response when questioned, was chilling. Did Ray have a duty to tell the judge and prosecutor his suspicions? How about Dallas? Ray's head started pounding, and all of a sudden he was very thirsty. As Ray walked up the stairs in the parking garage, he imagined a scotch over ice in a large glass.

Ray started up his Lexus and put the air conditioning on high. He pulled out of the parking garage and headed to the Veranda for a drink, but remembered Amber was cooking dinner at her place. He reluctantly passed the Veranda and pulled into the downtown convenience store parking lot. Beer would have to pacify him until he could drive to Amber's south Ft. Myers apartment, where he always kept a bottle of scotch. He went inside and purchased a six pack of Heineken as he tried to figure out how Helen set up the murder.

As he walked back to his car with a brown bag covering his beer, a police officer drove by and waved to Ray. He waved back as he opened his door and set the six pack on the passenger seat. He briefly considered the open container law as he grabbed a bottle. He looked down the road to make sure the officer wasn't doing a U-turn to investigate and was relieved to see the officer driving away to more pressing problems as he opened the beer.

The taste of beer was nice, but it was purely an appetizer. He needed some good twelve-year-old scotch to help him solve his ethical dilemma. As he drove south on U.S. 41, he played out the different scenarios in his mind. His first option would be to have a meeting with the judge and prosecutor in chambers and tell them of his suspicions. Of course, the only way to prove his theory was for him to be a witness for the defense. Spere would accuse him of trying to create a mistrial because of Dallas's poor performance on the stand. Judge Stalman would ask why he didn't bring it up before trial, and Ray would have to say he didn't know. But if he did that, was he confessing to malpractice because he hadn't done a thorough investigation into the case? If Dallas were convicted, could he sue Ray for malpractice?

Ray quickly finished his first bottle and started on the next. Ray considered the second scenario of reopening his case and calling Helen as a defense witness. He could subpoena her and make her testify. But Ray had tried years before to confuse Helen at a deposition and the subsequent trial. He wasn't able to shake her then and she damn well wasn't going to admit to a murder on the witness stand. After he was finished with her, Spere would get to cross-
194

examine Helen about their nasty divorce and argue that's the real reason Ray suggested she was a murderess. Ray was certain Spere would relish attacking Helen and making both of them look bad, especially after the sidebar conversation about Spere's black eyes. Ray's daughters would never forgive him for accusing their mother of murder.

Ray started on his next bottle as he considered the third scenario of doing nothing different than what he'd planned. His theory of defense from the beginning was that Bryce got killed by one of his lovers, or his lover's husband. When he started the trial, he didn't realize his theory of defense was actually what happened. He was just trying to muddy the waters and get his guilty client off by confusing the jury. Now he realized it wasn't just a theory; it was reality orchestrated by his ex-wife. At least, he thought that's what happened.

There were pros and cons for each scenario, and he needed to rest his tired and restless mind. He was looking forward to a relaxing evening with Amber and some well needed stress relief. As he parked his Lexus in front of her apartment, he told himself he needed to compartmentalize his life; it was time to leave the trial behind and enjoy Amber's company. As he walked to her door, he took a deep breath and decided to sleep on his decision. He knew from past experience that sleep was the great problem solver.

Amber lived in a new apartment complex with a gym, pool, and tennis courts. He thought about taking Amber for a late night swim after dinner and drinks. She'd always liked it before. He rang the door bell and thought of Amber's smile. A few seconds later, Amber answered the door and gave Ray a hug as she said, "I just saw the news report about the trial. It doesn't sound like things went well this afternoon."

"No, it didn't," Ray said as he walked toward the kitchen and his bottle of scotch. He could feel his tongue salivating as he got closer to his best friend.

Amber followed him into the kitchen. "I can't believe I took an afternoon off to go to the doctor and the juiciest part of the trial happens. They said Dallas got caught in some lies."

Ray poured the scotch over ice and took a belt before he answered. "It wasn't exactly a lie, but it sure looked bad in front of the jury. I told the son-of-a-bitch not to testify, but he insisted."

Amber leaned back against the counter. "He's the client; it's his decision."

Ray shrugged and took another belt. Amber lowered her voice. "You look tired, honey."

Ray cracked his neck. "I am. A lot of shit happened today, and I'm not sure how to handle it in closing argument tomorrow. There's no right answer, so I have to consider the least painful decision and what gives Dallas the best odds of an acquittal. Oh, and by the way, Beth got arrested at school today for having a joint."

Amber walked over and hugged Ray as she kissed him on the neck. Ray sighed and whispered, "That's nice."

Ray took another belt. "Would you like me to make you a drink?"

Amber smiled. "No. It looks like I'm not gonna be drinking anything for the next seven and a half months." Ray looked quizzically and asked, "What do you mean?" Amber squeezed Ray's arms and announced excitedly, "I'm pregnant. Can you believe it?"

Ray dropped his glass and it shattered on the tile.

Amber stepped back and looked dejected. "Are you mad?"

Ray asked in his best cross-examination voice, "I thought you were on the pill. You told me you were on the pill."

Amber crossed her arms. "Well, I was, but I missed a couple of days because my prescription ran out, and I didn't make it to the pharmacy. I didn't plan it; it just happened!"

Ray got another glass from the cabinet and made a drink in silence. Amber was getting angrier by the second. As Ray took another belt, she blurted out, "You're more concerned about your spilled drink than our baby!"

Ray raised his hands to his side and shook them as he asked angrily, "How do I know it's mine?"

Amber's face became sullen and she stared at Ray for five seconds before answering with clenched teeth, "You're a fucking asshole. Of course it yours; you're the only possibility."

Ray took another belt. "You told me you never wanted to have children because it would screw up your career. And now you trick me into this pregnancy, and you think I should be happy about it."

Amber shook her head. "I didn't trick you into it. It was a mistake, but now that it's happened, I'm excited about it. At least I was."

Ray finished his drink. "I've gotta go. I don't need this right now; I've got a lot of stuff to deal with."

Amber watched Ray walking toward the door and felt tears welling up in her eyes. She blurted out, "I thought you loved me."

Ray opened the door and looked back. "I loved the sexy reporter focused on her career. Besides, I already have a family."

Ray walked outside and shut the door. He immediately regretted what he said, but he was overwhelmed. He'd always heard that every man has a limit, but he always thought that was an excuse. Today, he'd found his limit, and he was losing it. He couldn't hold back his impulsive response to Amber's announcement and he couldn't focus. Ray's head was pounding with a headache, and he felt as helpless as a leaf floating down a stream.

Ray got into his Lexus and spun his tires as he left the parking lot. He'd not spun his tires since high school, but it felt really good. Ray was not ready to go home to his lonely house. He sped down U.S. 41 until he saw his favorite Irish pub, The Lucky Leprechaun. He pulled into the parking lot and slammed on his brakes, sliding into a parking space. As Ray was walking across the parking lot, his cell phone rang. He saw from the caller ID that Amber was calling. He turned his cell phone off and stuck it back in his pocket. It was time to drink.

Chapter 18

Thursday evening, 6:18 p.m.

Ray opened the mahogany door of The Lucky Leprechaun and heard the roar of a rowdy happy hour crowd. The building was originally a fast food restaurant that went out of business. The non-descript outer walls were a stucco finish, painted white with green trim. However, once you stepped inside it was like going back in time to an eighteenth century pub. The walls were old faded wood, imported from a demolished barn in the Irish countryside. All of the fixtures, fans, and beer taps were brass. All of the tables and chairs were antiques, made with wood pegs and tongue and grove joints. The only thing modern was the Bose sound system that constantly played Irish tunes.

Ray's eyes adjusted to the low light, and he looked around for a familiar face. As he scanned the bar, the bartender threw up his hand and smiled. Ray waved back and waded through the crowd toward the end of a bar with an open stool. The bartender's name was Percy O'Rourke and was a repeat client of Ray's.

Percy was a short man, but he was all muscle. He looked like he could easily lift a refrigerator and throw it. The latest case Ray had defended him on was a battery charge resulting from a fight in The Lucky Leprechaun's parking lot after hours. One of the bar customers had hung out in the parking lot after closing hours and was harassing one of the waitresses leaving work. The waitress called for Percy when he was emptying the trash. Percy ran over to the waitress and asked if she was alright. A fight broke out when the customers told Percy to mind his own business.

The customer ended up in the hospital with a broken jaw and a broken hand. The police investigated and arrested Percy because of his lengthy criminal record. Ray asked Percy at trial how the man's jaw and hand got broken. Percy pushed his dark unruly hair out of his eyes and answered, "The bloke hit me first in the ear and then my mouth. I don't know which one broke his hand, but I damn well know my right hand broke his jaw."

The jury acquitted Percy in five minutes.

Percy had two glasses of twelve-year-old scotch waiting for Ray when he reached the bar. Ray reached for his wallet and Percy held up his hand, yelling out above the noise, "Your money's no good here, counselor."

Ray thanked him and took a swallow. The scotch comforted Ray as it slid down his throat and into his belly. Percy walked down the bar to refill some beer pitchers with Guinness. Ray sat down on the bar stool, took another drink, and felt his tongue dance with pleasure. He could feel himself relaxing for the first time since he left the courthouse.

Behind Ray, a drunk man slurred, "Hey, it's the killer lawyer."

Ray turned and saw two lawyers he knew from downtown. Stan was a probate lawyer with a big firm, and Gary was a real estate lawyer who worked for a development company. Ray stood up as the two lawyers approached through the crowd. Ray was in no mood for polite chit-chat with casual acquaintances.

Stan said, "I was listening to the radio on the way here, and the news guy said your guy tanked on the witness stand. What happened?"

Ray shrugged. "Against my advice, he testified and got flambéed on cross. I told him not to testify, but he's a knowit-all."

Gary shrugged his shoulders and said, "Hell, the guy's guilty as sin. He just got caught in his lies."

Ray bristled. "I don't think Dallas did it."

Gary raised his eyebrows. "If he didn't do it, then who did?"

Ray took a belt and said casually, "An ex-girlfriend." Stan and Gary gave each other skeptical looks as Ray took another belt. Stan asked, "How are you gonna prove it?"

Ray took a deep breath. "That's a damn good question."

Someone on the other side of the bar started singing "Happy Birthday" to his girlfriend, and everyone joined in. Ray was glad for a break from the inquisitive lawyers. He didn't want to talk about the case, and he hoped they'd talk about something else, or he was going to walk away from their annoying questions.

After the song, Stan poked Ray in the arm and leaned toward him as he said in a lowered voice, "Come on, you can tell me. Your guy told you he did it, didn't he?"

Ray shook his head and looked over at Gary. "You know the difference between a prostitute and a probate lawyer?"

Gary shook his head and Stan stepped back, frowning.

Ray answered his own question. "A prostitute doesn't screw you when you're dead."

Gary laughed and Stan kept frowning. Ray picked up his drink and took the opportunity to leave the nosy lawyers. He snaked through the crowd toward the pool table. There were two bikers playing, so he took out a twenty and put it on edge of the table. He sat and drank, waiting his turn, and enjoying the swearing of the competing bikers. It was ten times better than sniveling lawyers trying to pick his brain.

Ray played pool and drank with the bikers for the next three hours. He lost $200 in bets to the bikers, but the mental diversion was worth every cent. When he left, he shook the bikers' hands, and gave them business cards for future use.

Ray walked over to the bar and thanked Percy for the drinks. It was time to go home and let Caesar out for his walk while he decided on his closing argument. He kept debating with himself whether Amber was pregnant with his child, or someone else's. He silently cursed himself for not getting a vasectomy after the divorce.

Chapter 19

Thursday evening, 11:04 p.m.

Ray pulled his Lexus out on U.S. 41 and headed to his house. As he was driving, his mind drifted to his ex-wife and her possible motive for murdering Bryce. It'd been some time since Bryce and Helen had dated, but there was a breakup and all of the angry emotions that went with it. It was hard to imagine Helen capable of murder, but the evidence was there. At least, it could be her. But what if she didn't do it and he publicly accused her of it? His daughters would never forgive him. Ray wasn't aware of any relationship between Dallas and Helen that would explain her setting him up for the murder.

A flashing blue light in Ray's mirror grabbed his attention and brought him back to reality. He pulled over at the next strip mall and felt his chest clench tight with anxiety. He reached into his console, searching for breath mints. He silently cursed himself as he realized he hadn't restocked his car since he ran out. He rolled down his window and said a silent prayer as the deputy approached from his cruiser.

The deputy shined his flashlight at Ray and all around the inside of the car as he said, "Give me your license and registration."

Ray said politely, "Certainly, officer."

Ray pulled out his wallet and retrieved his driver's license. He handed it to the officer and opened his glove compartment, retrieving his registration. He waited for the officer to finish reading his license and handed it to the officer. The officer said, "Stay in the car while I call these in."

"Yes, sir."

Ray wiped the sweat off of his brow as the officer walked back to his cruiser. Thankfully, he'd eaten some peanuts before he left The Lucky Leprechaun. Ray closed his eyes and prayed the peanuts hid the smell of scotch.

Ray promised God he'd quit drinking if the officer allowed him to continue home. He spent the next two minutes plea bargaining with God about his drinking and other bad habits. Ray could see the deputy approaching in his side mirror, and he took a deep breath.

The deputy pointed the flashlight at Ray and said, "Could you turn off your car and please step out of the vehicle?"

"Yes, officer." Ray got out of the vehicle and looked at the officer. "You're a lawyer, aren't you?"

Ray's stomach churned with bile. "Yes, I am."

The deputy asked, "Aren't you doing the Edison Home murder case this week?"

Ray felt a glimmer of hope. "Yes, it's been a busy week."

The deputy scratched his chin. "You were weaving in your lane. I guess you needed a few drinks to help you relax tonight."

Ray hesitated. If he denied he'd had anything to drink, the officer would know he was lying. If he admitted it, the officer may continue. Ray raised his eyebrows and gave a slight smile. "I had two drinks before dinner tonight."

The deputy smirked and said incredulously, "Two drinks, huh? They must've been the size of buckets."

Ray shrugged and said half-heartedly. "Scotch has a strong smell."

204

"I need you to do some field sobriety tests for me to determine whether or not you are impaired to operate your vehicle."

Ray knew it was very hard to pass these tests when the deputy already had an opinion that you're impaired. Ray convinced himself, like most drunks, that he could pass the tests. Ray answered, "Yes, officer. What do you want me to do?"

The deputy pointed to the painted line of a parking space. "I want you to walk ten steps forward, turn, and walk back."

Ray nodded and shuffled over to the line. He walked ten steps forward and tried to turn around, but lost his balance. He quickly stepped back on the line and said, "I'm alright. I'll walk back."

Ray returned the ten steps and looked at the officer. "What next?"

The officer stretched out his right arm and stuck out his pointer finger. "I want you to put your head back, close your eyes and touch your finger to the tip of your nose when I tell you."

Ray nodded and put his head back. He closed his eyes and immediately felt dizzy.
The deputy instructed, "Right hand first."

Ray slowly brought his finger forward and touched his upper lip.

"Left hand."

Ray concentrated and brought his finger forward, touching the middle of his nose and said excitedly, "I did it."

The deputy shook his head. "No, I said touch the tip. You touched the middle of the nose, so you failed the test." Ray pleaded. "Give me another test." "Say the alphabet backwards."

"Z, X, Y…wait a second. Let me start over."

The deputy shook his head. "No need; I've seen enough. You're under arrest for DUI. Please put your hands behind your back so I can handcuff you."

Ray pleaded, "I'm not drunk. Just follow me home; I'll be OK."

The officer replied firmly, "Put your hands behind your back, or I'll also arrest you for resisting arrest."

Ray was sober enough to know he should follow directions at this point and put his hands behind his back. The officer handcuffed Ray and led him to the cruiser, opening the rear door. As Ray squatted to get in the back seat, the deputy put his hand on Ray's head and guided him as he said, "You need to get in the back so I can ask you some questions.

"Watch your head."

Ray maneuvered into the back seat and felt nauseous. He needed to be at home preparing for closing argument, but he realized he was going to be spending the night in jail. Maybe he could request the same cell as Dallas. His head started pounding as he pictured the newspaper headlines and his mug shot spread out on the newspaper and television news. He thought about Caesar at home, trying to hold it in. He thought about lecturing Beth about her pot arrest on the same day he got arrested for DUI. He wondered if Amber would do a report on his arrest. After considering Amber's reporter instincts, Ray concluded she would demand to cover his arrest—especially after their last meeting.

The officer got into the driver's seat and radioed in the arrest. He turned and looked at Ray. "I'm requesting you take a breathalyzer. If you don't take it, your license will be suspended for one year.

Ray answered quietly, "I'll take it."

Chapter 20

Friday morning, 12:20 a.m.

The police cruiser pulled into the sally port at the jail, and the mechanical door creaked as it came down. The door was made of horizontal bars spaced six inches apart. It allowed air into the sally port, but secured the area before the arresting officer opened the rear door and let out the arrestee. The deputy unlocked the handcuffs and led Ray into a small room with a breathalyzer on the table. It smelled of stale urine and dried vomit. He sat down in a rusting metal chair and motioned for Ray to do the same in a matching chair in front of the breathalyzer.

Ray had defended DUI cases for twenty years, but he'd never seen a breathalyzer up close. It was a gray machine with a protruding cylinder holding a thick straw about four inches long. Ray knew for the machine to work he had to blow hard at least five seconds for the machine to properly register the alcohol content in his breath. If you didn't blow long enough, or hard enough, the machine would print out "deficient sample" on the breath card. Ray had observed many DUI defendants win cases by blowing slightly into the machine, and when the machine printed "deficient sample" claim the machine was broken. During the ride to the jail, Ray had decided that was his strategy.

The deputy pointed at the breathalyzer and said authoritatively, "Lean forward and blow deeply into the straw until you see the red light on the machine light up. Keep blowing until I say quit."

Ray nodded and leaned toward the machine. He put his

lips around the straw and faked blowing into the straw for about fifteen seconds. He stopped and looked over at the officer. "It's not working."

The deputy smirked and raised his voice. "Alright, Mr. Lawyer. Stop playing games and blow into the straw, or I'm gonna write down that you refused to blow. Now blow until the light comes on."

Ray pleaded. "I'm not refusing to blow; the machine is broken."

The deputy held up his pointer finger and said gruffly, "I'm giving you one more shot. Now do it."

Ray faked his blow a second time.

The deputy turned off the breathalyzer and shook his head angrily as he said. "That's it. You've refused to follow instructions; your license will be suspended for one year automatically."

Ray leaned back in his chair and took a deep breath. He knew his license would be suspended for a DUI conviction anyway. At this point, he was trying to avoid giving the police any more evidence than they already had. The police officer finished up his paperwork and closed his files as Ray thought about Caesar trying to hold it in.

The deputy stood up and pointed as he said, "Stand up and walk back out to the fingerprint station."

Ray complied and walked in front of the shatterproof glass separating the sally port from the air-conditioned control center with large windows. As he walked toward the fingerprint station, he saw the shift supervisor pointing him out to some junior officers. They all looked at Ray and laughed knowingly.

After Ray was fingerprinted, he was led into the booking room and his mug shot was taken. Ray knew this photograph would immediately be given to all of the TV stations for their morning newscast. Ray thought it would be ironic if Amber was given the job of reporting the story since her pregnancy news started his drunk fest at The Lucky Leprechaun. The deputy sarcastically told him to smile. The bright lights and flash of the camera increased the pounding of his headache.

The police officer motioned toward a small room with a single chair, small table, and phone. "Go make your one phone call. And don't call Dominoes; we don't allow delivery." The deputy laughed at his old standby line.

Ray walked in and grabbed the phone. He called Doug's cell phone and hoped he'd answer.

After four rings, Doug answered groggily, "Hello?"

Ray pleaded, "Doug, this is Ray. You gotta help me. I fucked up and got arrested for DUI."

Doug was waking up. "Oh, shit."

Ray spoke rapidly, "I've got closing arguments at nine tomorrow morning."

Doug chided, "You know they won't let you out until first appearance tomorrow morning."

Ray was resigned to his fate. "I know. But Judge Stalman's office opens at 8:30. I need you to be there and explain to his judicial assistant what's happened and that I might be late. Oh, and could you go by my house and let Caesar out. You remember where I have my key hidden, right?"

Doug said, "I remember. I'll take care of it."

"Thanks, Doug."

Ray hung up the phone and walked back into the hallway. The deputy led Ray to a large holding cell forty feet wide by sixty feet deep. It housed everyone that had been arrested that day and was waiting for a judge to set bond at first appearance. There looked to be at least fifty men inside, some sitting on stainless benches and some asleep on the floor. There was one stainless commode that a man was puking into. A stainless sink was next to the commode and another inmate was using it as a urinal. A stainless water fountain next to the sink was overflowing because of a clogged drain. Everyone inside looked up as the door creaked open and Ray walked in.

The deputy slammed the cell shut behind Ray. "Have a good night. They'll set your bond tomorrow morning."

One of the inmates looked at Ray and asked loudly, "Why are you wearing a suit and tie?"

Ray noticed some of the inmates looking over at him menacingly. He thought quickly, because he was in no mood for a confrontation. "I buried my mom today and went to a bar. The fucking cops arrested me for DUI."

The other inmates looked satisfied and said nothing. Ray walked over to a corner of the cell and took off his coat. He sat down on the floor and loosened his tie while he thought of Caesar stuck at home. His neighbor had stopped by in the afternoon and let him out. Caesar would've held it as long as possible, but he'd probably already gone inside the house. He was sure Caesar had water, but he had to be hungry by now. Ray felt very guilty about abandoning Caesar and disappointing his children. Ray knew Julie would be disappointed with both him and her sister.

Ray shifted his thoughts to Amber. She was the last woman in the world he thought would accidentally get pregnant. She was always bad-mouthing her college friends that got married and started a family rather than advance in their careers. Now, she was pregnant and wanted to start a family with Ray.

Ray thought of his marriage to Helen. It had started out great and he was convinced they'd be together forever. He loved his daughters and spent all of his money keeping Helen and the girls in the latest fashions. He always took them on trips and bought them expensive gifts. Unfortunately, his meager savings was quickly drained, and he started running up the credit card bills. He never complained to Helen, but he started working longer hours, trying to bring in more money. He started drinking more, and the fights started when he came home drunk. Helen had her affair with Larry and divorced him soon after.

Even though Helen had divorced him, he'd never gotten over her. At least until today when he realized she was capable of murder and setting up an innocent man. Or maybe not?

He loved his daughters and missed being around them every day. How would they react if he had another child? Would they be angry, or would they like another sister? Or maybe a brother? Maybe his family name would be carried on to another generation? Maybe God was giving him a second chance at being a father? Maybe he'd be a better husband and father this time around.

Ray was brought back to reality by a yelling match between two inmates arguing over a bench. One said he'd been there the longest and was entitled to it. The other one eloquently argued that was the bench he always slept on when he'd been arrested. They finally split apart and went to opposite sides of the large cell. Ray suddenly realized he was mentally and physically exhausted. He rolled up his coat into a makeshift pillow and lay down on the floor. He was sleeping within fifteen seconds.

Chapter 21

Friday morning, 8:40 a.m.

The head bailiff opened Dallas's cell at the jail and asked, "Are you ready for the big finale?"

Dallas nodded. "I hope my lawyer has got a good closing argument. I don't think I did too good on the stand yesterday."

Dallas held out his hands, and the head bailiff handcuffed him for the walk from the jail, through a hidden hallway with no doors or windows, to the holding cell by the courtroom. As they were walking down the hallway Dallas asked, "What do you think about the trial?"

The head bailiff shrugged. "I've seen juries convict people I thought were innocent and I've seen them walk some scumbags I thought were guilty as sin. You never know."

Dallas squeaked. "That's comforting."

The head bailiff didn't answer, and they walked down a long hallway toward the holding cell, next to the courtroom. As they were walking, Dallas remembered his analysis of the possible suspects at the Edison Home fundraiser that were mad at him. Ray's investigator had gotten a list of all the guests that bought tickets to the party. Dallas had calculated there were twenty-six people at the party that had a motive to set him up for murder. They were his third ex-wife, and two ex-girlfriends, nine investors that lost money, and fourteen people he screwed in business deals.

Helen was one of the people he'd screwed in a business

deal, but he'd asked acquaintances, and was told she was there with her husband. How could she have killed Bryce and planted the gun at his house while she was with her husband? Dallas had no proof that Helen did it, and he didn't want his lawyer mad at him for saying his ex-wife was a murderer. In addition, Dallas had convinced himself he would be acquitted, and he didn't want to lose his real estate broker's license for promising rebate cash in bags. He would have to testify about Helen's motive for the murder. If he were acquitted, his testimony would be transcribed and sent to the Florida Real Estate Commission, and he would have his license revoked for unethical behavior.

Since Dallas had been in custody, his real estate brokerage firm had gone downhill. The six salesmen had left and gone with other brokers. At the time of his arrest, he had three real estate developments in the planning stage. All three developments folded when the banks pulled his financing.

Dallas had refinanced his house to pay his legal bills. The only person on his payroll was his secretary, who collected rent from his strip mall and his commercial rentals. It was a very small income stream after expenses, but it had been enough to keep the doors open. If Dallas was acquitted, he'd return to a business on life support, but at least it had a steady pulse.

Dallas thought back to the night of the Edison Home fundraiser. He'd arrived stag because he was more concerned with schmoozing with his current investors and trying to recruit new investors than he was with trying to impress a date. He had arrived early and was drinking with a few investors at the bar under the banyan tree, when Bryce Cervante had shown up. He lost his cool and caused a scene with Cervante over the lost land deal.

The police had escorted him to his car and he'd driven home. He ordered a pizza and watched basketball until late. He woke up the next morning rested and was reading the paper when the police knocked on his door. From that point on, he'd lived a nightmare.

Dallas had been housed on the fourth floor for his entire eight months behind bars. He'd luckily managed to avoid Julio during his time there. All of the other accused murderers and high-risk inmates were housed there. These anti-social individuals mixed like oil and water, and there were always fights on the floor. The jailers had nicknamed the fourth floor the "gladiator floor" because of the large number of fights. Dallas had avoided disputes and stayed to himself, but every night he dreamed of being attacked by a younger, stronger man with nothing to lose.

** ** ** ** **

The bailiff unlocked the heavy metal door of the holding cell next to the courtroom, and Dallas walked in. He was surprised to see Ray sitting on the stainless bench in a rumpled suit.

Dallas asked warily, "What are you doing on this side?"

Ray stood up. "I got arrested for DUI last night. I'm sorry."

Dallas sat down on the bench and sighed. "I guess you didn't do too much on my case last night."

Ray said, "One of the reasons I got drunk was that I realized during the trial that you didn't do it. It really bothered me, and then my girlfriend told me she's pregnant. The pressure got to me, and next thing I know, I'm in a police cruiser."

Dallas gave an incredulous look. "Are you telling me before the trial you thought I did it?"

Ray shrugged. "I didn't know. But after hearing all the evidence, I'm sure you didn't do it."

Dallas considered Ray's proclamation. "Well, that makes me feel good. Do you think you can convince the jury?"

Ray nodded. "I'll try."

"Maybe we should ask for a continuance for a day, so you can go home and shower, and spend some more time preparing."

Ray shrugged. "I'll ask, but I don't know if the judge will do it."

The assistant bailiff walked in and handed Dallas his street clothes for the trial. The assistant bailiff looked at Ray and slowly shook his head and stated matter-of-factly, "I guess you're already dressed."

After the assistant bailiff left, Ray ran his hands through his hair and said, "I'm sorry. I should've been drinking at home, reviewing my notes."

Dallas began putting on his street clothes. "It's OK, Ray. I picked you to be my attorney for two reasons. The first reason was your ex-wife had a fling with Bryce, so I knew you'd dig up all the dirt you could on him. I also knew you'd do everything you could to trash him in the media and in court. So far, I've been very pleased with everything that's come out about Bryce."

Ray sighed. "I still shouldn't have been out drinking."

Dallas laughed ruefully as he buttoned up his shirt. "Two years ago, I was playing golf with a buddy of mine, and I asked him who the best criminal defense attorney was

218

in town. He told me it was you, when you weren't drinking. I asked him who the second best was, and he told me it was you, when you were drinking."

Ray felt his face flush, but said nothing. Dallas lamented, "I hope he was right."

There was an awkward silence for a few seconds and Ray asked quietly, "What was the second reason you hired me?"

Dallas smiled. "I wanted a killer lawyer."

Ray winced. He started to protest about his unwanted moniker, but he thought better of it. He finally said, "I'll do my best for you."

Dallas glared at Ray and snarled, "Your best isn't good enough; you better win. If I'm convicted, I'm gonna sue you for legal malpractice."

Chapter 22

Friday morning, 9:18 a.m.

The head bailiff opened the heavy metal door of the holding cell and handed Ray his belt and tie. "We didn't want Dallas's lawyer to commit suicide right before closing arguments. We would've had to declare a mistrial and do all of this again."

Ray looked at the jovial head bailiff and wondered how many other jokes had been told that morning in the courthouse at his expense. "Thanks."

The head bailiff handed Dallas his belt. Dallas had elected to wear a suit with no tie during the trial. He felt it made his look more causal, and therefore, less worried to the jury. Ray had learned a long time ago that trying to dress defendants up in ties didn't work if they were tugging at the tie and fidgeting during the trial. Ray thought it was kind of like putting perfume on a pig—it'll never fool anybody, and it'll just irritate the pig.

The head bailiff held the door open and motioned both of them to the courtroom. "The judge told me that both of you should go to counsel table until he takes the bench. And then he'll address the DUI."

Ray's heart fluttered as he walked down the short hallway and rounded the corner to a whispering courtroom. As soon as he walked into the courtroom, all of the whispering stopped. He looked through the crowd of spectators and saw Doug sitting next to Amber on the back row. He nodded toward them, but neither one was smiling. Ray sat down at the defense table and glanced at Dallas, his face pale with fear.

The head bailiff announced, "All rise. The Honorable Gary Stalman is presiding over this court."

Judge Stalman walked in and sat down. "Everyone be seated."

Judge Stalman waited until everyone sat down and the courtroom was quiet again. "Mr. Harrison, please stand and approach the bench."

Ray stood up and walked awkwardly to the podium. He felt dizzy, but took a deep breath and looked up at Judge Stalman.

Judge Stalman said, "Mr. Harrison, you were arrested last night for DUI. I have spoken with the first appearance judge, and she has agreed to allow me to conduct your first appearance. I've read the officer's booking sheet and note that, according to court records, you have no prior arrests. Therefore, I am releasing you on your own recognizance. However, you should know that before I took the bench I reported you to the Florida Bar for conduct unbecoming a lawyer during trial. I'm sure the Bar will be conducting their investigation and deciding on an appropriate punishment."

Judge Stalman took a breath and glanced over his reading glasses. "We have finished your first appearance. Now, return to counsel table and resume your job as defense lawyer for the accused."

Ray's ears were pounding with blood as he walked slowly to the defense table and sat down. Dallas glared at Ray and turned to look at the spectators. He saw two friends give him the thumbs up sign, but he didn't feel any better.

Judge Stalman looked over at the prosecutor. "Are you ready for closing arguments?"

Spere jumped up. "Of course, Judge."

Judge Stalman turned toward Ray, "How about the defense?"

Dallas nudged Ray, and he stood up. Ray's voice cracked. "Judge, I'm asking for a one day continuance so I can deal with my personal problems and prepare for closing argument. My client also wants me to have a day to get my affairs in order. I would feel much better prepared with a one day continuance."

Judge Stalman was in all of his glory. "Your motion is denied. We're going to take a fifteen minute break and then come back for closing arguments. I suggest you use this time wisely."

Judge Stalman stood up quickly, and the bailiff announced, "All rise."

Judge Stalman walked off the bench, and Ray sat down. The head bailiff motioned for Dallas to come with him to the holding cell. As Dallas stood up he whispered to Ray in an urgent voice, "Remember what I said."

Ray nodded soberly and watched Dallas being led back to the holding cell. Ray looked at his table and saw it was completely empty. The file on the case was locked in his Lexus which had been towed from his DUI arrest location. He couldn't get it back until he went and paid the tow and storage bill. Ray knew the case, but it was very unnerving not having his file. He could hear people moving in the courtroom and talking. He dreaded running the gauntlet of reporters to get outside, but knew there was no other way.

Ray stood up and walked uneasily out through the wooden swinging gate separating the audience area from the attorney area. A young reporter shoved the morning paper toward him and asked, "What do you think of the headline?"

Ray looked at the paper and read KILLER LAWYER
ARRESTED FOR DUI.

Ray said quietly, "No comment."

Another reporter shouted, "Have you been drunk the
entire trial?"

Ray ignored him and walked toward the rear door in
the courtroom. A newspaper reporter yelled, "Are you still
sleeping with the blonde TV reporter?"

Ray turned around and glared at the reporter. He
moved toward him and yelled, "That's none of your
business."

Ray was grabbed from behind and he whirled around to
see Doug, who whispered, "Let's go to the bathroom.
Come on, you don't need this."

Ray nodded and Doug released him. Ray followed
Doug out of the courtroom as he plowed through the noisy
reporters, clearing a path. Ray said nothing as they walked
down the hallway and around the corner to the bathroom.
Amber was waiting outside the bathrooms, glaring at Ray.

Doug patted Ray on the back and whispered, "I'll stay
here to keep the reporters away."

Ray nodded. "Thanks."

Ray walked to Amber and reached for her hands. She
stepped back and put her hands on her hips as she said,
"No, Ray. You need to listen; I've decided to have an
abortion. Doug is driving me to the clinic as soon as I leave
here."

Ray stood still and stared at Amber, looking for a sign
of weakness. He saw no change in her expression and
finally said, "I was wrong last night. I've thought about it,
and I want to have the baby with you."

Amber shook her head. "No Ray, that's not true. My
mom always told me, 'In the wine lies the truth.' Last night

you said exactly what you thought."

Ray pleaded and his voice cracked. "Don't I have a say in this?"

Amber gave him a bitter smile. "No, Ray, you don't. As you noted so eloquently last night, I'm a career woman that doesn't have time for a baby."

Ray started to tear up, but quickly wiped it away. Amber shook her head in disgust and walked away as she said, "Give me a break."

Ray turned and watched Amber walk by Doug and heard her say, "I'll wait for you outside."

Doug walked slowly up to Ray and motioned with his head toward the bathroom. They walked into the bathroom, and Doug locked the door while Ray walked over to the sink. He washed his hands and then his face while Doug waited in silence. Ray finally looked in the mirror at Doug while he was drying his hands and asked, "Why are you driving her to the clinic?"

Doug cleared his throat. "Ray, I know you're mad, but I'm doing you a favor. Do you really want to raise a kid with this shark? You'll be fucking miserable for the rest of your life. Trust me."

Ray ran his hands through his hair. "I don't know, Doug. So much is happening at once; I'm having problems dealing with it."

Doug nodded. "I bet."
There was loud knocking at the door and shouts to open up.

Ray gathered his thoughts. "Thanks for telling Judge Stalman and getting me brought over."

"No problem. Oh, by the way, I stopped by and let Caesar out and fed him."

"Thanks."

Doug raised his voice, "Ray, you've got to suck it up. All week you made a lot of points with the jury and the evidence is weak. You've still got a chance here. Forget about Amber and the DUI. Go in there and do your thing."

Ray nodded. "You're right."

Doug stepped toward the door and said quietly, "Amber's waiting."

Ray waved half-heartedly and Doug unlocked the bathroom and left. Ray walked over and locked it back for privacy. He had six minutes before the judge was coming back out and he damn well didn't want to be late. He looked at himself in the mirror and shook his head. He wondered how Dallas felt in the holding cell, pondering his alcoholic lawyer's ability to perform while hung over. He laughed to himself for the first time in a few days as he realized he'd done many closing arguments hung over.

Ray took a deep breath as he looked in the mirror and straightened his tie. It was show time. Ray unlocked the door and walked back to the courtroom, ignoring reporters and curious glances from courthouse workers. He sat down at the defense table and looked over at Spere, who chuckled and shook his head. Ray closed his eyes and concentrated until he heard footsteps approaching his table. He opened his eyes and saw Dallas walking in front of him. He gave the thumbs up sign and Dallas smiled.

The head bailiff announced, "All rise. The Honorable Gary Stalman is presiding over this court."

Judge Stalman walked in and sat down. He glanced around the courtroom, looking for any quick sitters. "You may be seated. Bailiff, bring in the jury."

After the jury came in and got comfortable, Judge Stalman announced, "The State will make the first argument and the defense will follow. Are you ready Mr.
226

Spere?

Spere stood up. "Yes, Your Honor."

As Spere approached the podium, Ray heard the main door to the courtroom creaking open. He turned, hoping Amber had changed her mind and come to watch his closing argument. Helen walked in with their two daughters and sat down in the back row. His girls gave him a small wave and smiled. Helen didn't look at Ray.

Spere said, "Ladies and gentlemen, the State thanks you for your jury service. I know it's been a long week and you've made a sacrifice being here away from your families and your jobs. Jury service is a civic responsibility that most Americans cherish. The State welcomes the obligation to prove our case beyond a reasonable doubt to a jury of the defendant's peers."

Spere hesitated and looked at his notes. "The State has charged first degree murder against the defendant. That means we have alleged the defendant murdered the victim in a premeditated design. Let's first look at the victim, Bryce Cervante. He's a hometown boy made good; he grew up here and returned after college and law school. He had a successful real estate law firm, specializing in legal problems associated with developments. As far as his personal life goes, he liked the ladies and everyone here in town knew that. Don't hold this vice against him, because it had nothing to do with his murder. His murder is about one thing: revenge."

Spere turned and pointed to Dallas. "The defendant shot Bryce Cervante for revenge. Pure and simple revenge. The defendant spent $500,000 on legal fees with Mr. Cervante and felt Mr. Cervante betrayed him. There are 500,000 reasons the defendant pumped two bullets through Mr. Cervante's heart and watched him bleed."

Spere walked over toward the defense table and stared at Dallas. After a few seconds, he turned back to the jury and lowered his voice. "But the defendant was smart. He knew people had seen him argue with Mr. Cervante at the beginning of the party. He knew people would assume he was the murderer. So, he thought. He planned. He premeditated how he could get away with the murder of his sworn enemy. He came up with an ingenious plan where he'd make the murder appear to be related to Bryce's well-known amorous ways."

Spere walked over to the clerk's table and picked up the murder weapon, wrapped in a plastic evidence bag. He walked back to the podium and held up the gun. "Let's look at further evidence of premeditation: no serial number. The defendant had been planning the murder before the night of the party. He'd bought a gun from the streets and ground off the serial number to make it untraceable. Think about it. His first conscious choice of murder was to purchase the weapon. His second choice was to file off the serial number. His third choice was to use gloves when loading the bullets into the gun, so there'd be no fingerprints. All of these choices were made before the night he murdered Bryce Cervante."

Spere sat the gun down on the podium. "Let's talk about the night of the murder. The defendant got to the party early and waited on Mr. Cervante, like a predator stalking his prey. As soon as he walked up to the bar with a crowd of people, the defendant ambushed him so there'd be a fight with a lot of witnesses and a police escort off the property. What a great group of witnesses to prove you had started a fight and been sent away from the scene of the murder. He could claim he was set up by another enemy of Bryce Cervante. What a plan. What premeditation."

228

Dallas slammed his hands down on the counsel table, stood up and yelled, "That's bullshit!"

The head bailiff and two assistant bailiffs rushed toward Dallas, and he instinctively put his hands in front of him.

Judge Stalman screamed, "Bind him and gag him."

The muscular, gray-haired head bailiff pulled his Taser, pointed it at Dallas's chest, and commanded, "Sit down and shut up."

Dallas sat down quickly and realized he'd made a huge mistake. He looked over at Ray for guidance. Ray put his index finger to his mouth and quietly told Dallas to calm down. One of the assistant bailiffs went to a closet in the hallway to the holding cell and pulled out the supplies for such a situation. He walked back in the courtroom with a bag and a body chain. The first assistant bailiff gave the bag to the second assistant bailiff and then headed for Dallas.

The head bailiff with the Taser aimed it at Dallas and said firmly, "Stand up and walk to the side of the table."

Dallas obliged. The assistant bailiff with the chains walked up to Dallas with the multiple chains rattling. He put the first chain around the waist and locked it down. A second chain was attached to the waist chain with two ankle clamps at the bottom. The assistant bailiff put these clamps around Dallas's ankles and said, "Put your hands in front of your waist."

Dallas obliged. The assistant bailiff grabbed a third chain with handcuffs and fastened them. He then attached the other end of the chain to the waist chain with a padlock. The head bailiff with the Taser said, "Sit back down and open your mouth."

The second assistant bailiff walked in front of Dallas

and commanded, "Keep your mouth open while I put this handkerchief inside."

Dallas looked over at Ray, who nodded. Dallas opened his mouth wide, and the bailiff stuffed a white handkerchief inside and tied a red handkerchief on top of Dallas's mouth and cinched the knot behind his head. Dallas looked over at Ray with wide eyes, but didn't move his body.

Judge Stalman said, "If you disrupt my courtroom again, you'll be removed and we'll continue the trial without you."

Dallas gave a brief nod. Ray stood up and asked, "May we approach?"

"Yes, you may."

As Ray walked to the sidebar, he saw Spere grinning. Ray lowered his voice, "Your Honor, I have to object to my client being bound and gagged in front of the jury. I suggest the bailiffs remove the bindings, and I guarantee my client will not make another outburst."

Judge Stalman said loudly, "Objection overruled. Maybe if you had counseled your client on how to act in closing argument last night instead of going out drinking, we wouldn't have this problem."

Ray glared at Judge Stalman, who glared back before asking sarcastically, "Anything else, counselor?"

Ray ground his teeth. "No, Your Honor."

Ray sat down, and Spere returned to the podium before politely asking, "May I continue, Your Honor?"

"You may."

Spere raised his voice. "Ladies and gentlemen, I'm glad you were able to see the defendant when he's angry. He almost looked angry enough to murder me."

Ray stood up. "Objection."

Judge Stalman pointed at Spere. "Sustained. Talk about

the evidence in the case, Mr. Spere."

Spere nodded and continued. "After the defendant was thrown out of the party, he went home, put on gloves, and grabbed the murder weapon, along with rope and bungee cords to secure his prey. He drove back downtown and parked a few blocks from the Edison Home so he wouldn't be seen. He walked back and hid in the bushes, next to the sidewalk that led to the pier. He knew it was a popular spot for party-goers that wanted some fresh air. He laid in wait for his prey.

"Unfortunately for Bryce Cervante, he walked along that sidewalk to get away from the party and admire the view of the river. The defendant jumped out of the bushes and surprised Mr. Cervante with the gun. The defendant ordered him into the garage and shut the door for the privacy he needed for his well-planned assassination.

"He ordered Mr. Cervante to strip down and get in the driver's seat of the Model T Ford. He threw the bungee cords at Mr. Cervante and ordered him to wrap his hands around the steering wheel to disable him so he could finish with the rope. The defendant wrapped Mr. Cervante with the rope while holding him at gunpoint. I'm sure he stood back and admired his handiwork before the *coup de grace*. He'd gotten Bryce into a sexually compromised position, so the police would assume one of his lovers' husbands or boyfriends killed him in a jealous rage."

Spere pulled the gun from the plastic bag by the handle. He pointed the gun at the podium and lowered it slowly as he said, "The defendant inched forward, savoring the moment, and jammed the gun into Mr. Cervante's skin to silence the noise. Remember, we know the gun was touching the skin because of the stippling that ripped into the victim's skin, according to the medical examiner's testimony. The defendant looked into his eyes and pulled the trigger twice. Bryce Cervante's life leaked out of him as the defendant smiled."

Spere put the gun back into the bag and walked to the clerk's table, setting it down. He walked slowly back to the podium as he stared at Dallas. Ray could hear a low, guttural noise coming from Dallas, like a dog awakened at night by a strange sound.

When Spere reached the podium he spoke quietly. "It was a good plan. The defendant walked back to his car and hid the gun beneath the seat. The defendant made his getaway from the scene of the crime without anyone seeing him and threw his gloves out the window on the way home. Unfortunately for the defendant, his euphoria made him forget about the gun. He left it in his car, and we found it the next morning."

Spere pointed to Dallas and said, "The defendant planned to execute Bryce Cervante. He followed his meticulous plan and almost got away with it. Sometimes smart criminals don't remember everything. Dallas Kelley is guilty of first degree murder."

Spere looked at Judge Stalman and said quietly, "The State rests, Your Honor."

Chapter 23

Friday morning, 10:29 a.m.

Judge Stalman looked at Ray. "Mr. Harrison, your turn."

Ray walked to the podium without any notes and cleared his throat. "Ladies and gentlemen, Dallas and I would like to thank you for your attention this week to the evidence. I know it's been a long week for everyone, but we're getting near the end of the trial. After the judge reads the jury instructions to you, you will retire to the jury room and decide whether or not Dallas is a murderer."

Ray hesitated, turned, and pointed to Dallas. "I want everyone to look at Dallas Kelley."

Everyone in the courtroom turned and stared at Dallas, as directed. He looked guilty as hell with the chains and gag over his mouth. Ray waited a few seconds before continuing. "My client apologizes to you for his outburst. And you can see he has paid dearly for his impulsive display of emotions."

Ray turned back and faced the jury. "But, I want you to ask yourself what should an innocent man do when lies are being told about him in open court? Do you sit there and let the slander continue? Do you keep silent and let an intellectual midget say outrageous lies without any proof?"

Spere burst to his feet. "Objection."

"Sustained. This is argument. No more name calling, Mr. Harrison."

"What proof do they have?" Ray asked as he slowly looked at every juror, "They have the murder weapon found in my client's car. My client's car was not locked, and his fingerprints were not on the murder weapon. There was no gunshot residue on my client's hands. The prosecutor makes up this story that my client had this masterful plan and he was this cunning assassin, but he left the murder weapon where it could be found. It's a logically inconsistent theory, and it's ridiculous."

Ray walked to the side of the podium and looked at every juror before he continued. "I submit to you that a more logical explanation is that someone planted the gun in my client's car after killing the victim. Anyone at the Edison Home fundraiser saw the fight between Dallas and Bryce and knew he'd be a suspect. There was a lot of planning to this murder, but it was not my client doing the planning."

Ray stopped and took a deep breath. "If not Dallas, then who was the real murderer? Who had a motive and an opportunity to kill Bryce Cervante? Who had the intelligence and bait to lure a man to a secluded area of the Edison Home, get him to take off his clothes, and tie him up without yelling or a struggle? Who was it? Or should I say, who was she?"

Ray stepped to the side of the podium as he considered whether to turn and look at Helen. Maybe she'd flee the courtroom or stand and yell at Ray. Maybe she'd do nothing and his daughters would never talk to him again for embarrassing their mother in a cheap courtroom gimmick to confuse the jury and get his client off. Ray decided on the shotgun approach.

"How many ex-lovers of Bryce Cervante were at the Edison Home fundraiser? Well, we know of at least three, and I presented them to you at trial. Who knows how many other ex-lovers were there that night. Ten? Twenty?"

Ray turned and pointed at Spere. "The burden of proof is on the State. They should've investigated all of Bryce Cervante's ex-lovers that were at this fundraiser and witnessed the fight between Bryce and Dallas. If she were mad at Bryce and wanted him dead, she needed to point the finger elsewhere. What a perfect target. All she'd have to do is wipe her fingerprints from the gun and take it to Dallas's house and plant it. If the car was locked, she could've put it in the garbage can or thrown it in the bushes. Yes, she planned the murder very well."

Spere stood up. "Objection, speculation, Your Honor."

Judge Stalman said, "Overruled. This is argument counsel; you're supposed to speculate what the evidence means. Sit down."

Spere timidly returned to his seat. Ray walked over to the clerk's table and picked up photographs. As he walked back to the podium he said, "I want you to look at these photographs. Look at how the victim was tied up. You heard the first witness on the scene, the maintenance worker, tell you there was no sign of a struggle. What is the most logical explanation of no struggle? The prosecution's version is that my client waited in the bushes with a gun near the sidewalk and hoped Bryce Cervante would come strolling, by himself, at that exact time and he wouldn't put up a struggle as his sworn enemy had him strip down and tied him to a car seat, while a gun was held to his head.

"Remember, the first officer on the scene wrote in his report that the victim had a smile on his face. If your sworn enemy has stripped you down and tied you to a car seat with a gun pointed at your head, you don't have a smile on your face. A more logical explanation is that one of Bryce's exlovers lured him to the secluded garage for a sexual encounter. Apparently, the victim had a kinky taste for foreplay that involved bondage and, as I proved with Karen Gilmore, an appetite for oral sex. That would explain the lack of a struggle. It would also explain how the victim allowed a gun to touch his skin without a struggle. Maybe he never saw the gun in the darkness. Maybe his eyes were focused on something more alluring than his lover's hand. Maybe his eyes were closed in ecstasy."

Ray looked all of the jurors in the eyes again. He raised his left index finger on his left hand and said, "Remember, the medical examiner's assistant testified that he smelled jasmine on the body. Maybe the killer was wearing jasmine perfume."

Ray walked to the other side of the podium and let his theory sink in. "What did Bryce Cervante do to his ex-lover to force her into a murderous rage? We may never know. However, we do know that Hell hath no fury like a woman scorned."

Spere stood up. "Objection."

Judge Stalman shook his head. "Overruled."

Ray grabbed the podium with both hands and lowered his voice. "Maybe he called her the wrong name. Maybe she offered to leave her husband and move in with him, and he refused. Maybe he backed out on a prearranged vacation or some financial commitment with his lover. Or maybe a jealous husband walked in on his wife pleasuring the victim and he snapped. He pulled a gun and jammed it into the victim's chest before pulling the trigger. The killer's wife was overcome with guilt and fear of her own involvement and hasn't come forward to turn her husband into the police. All of these scenarios are possible and match the physical evidence at the scene of the crime. Therefore, if you don't know, the State hasn't proven their case beyond a reasonable doubt."

Ray walked over to the defense table and pointed at Dallas. "Do we have an innocent man sitting at this table or a calculating murderer with bad luck?"

Ray walked back to the podium and leaned forward, resting on his elbows. "That's a hard question, isn't it? Remember, the burden of proof is on the State. If you're back in the jury room and you say to yourself, maybe he did it, that's not enough. If you're back in the jury room and you say to yourself, he possibly did it, that's not enough. If you're back in the jury room and you say to yourself, he probably did it, that's not enough. You have to know, beyond all reasonable doubt, that he did it."

Ray walked to the side of the podium. "The judge is going to give you some instructions on reasonable doubt. I believe he's going to tell you a reasonable doubt can come from the evidence, conflict in the evidence, or a lack of evidence. He's also going to tell you that if you waiver or vacillate in your deliberations, that means the State hasn't proved their case, and you must find the defendant not guilty."

Ray lowered his voice. "Think about that. The mere fact that while you are deliberating, if you waiver or vacillate, this means the State hasn't proven their case beyond all reasonable doubt, and you must find the defendant not guilty. Remember, at the beginning of the trial you took an oath to follow the law."

Ray walked back behind the podium. "I'd like to point out a conflict in the evidence and the lack of evidence. The biggest conflict is the result of the gun shot residue test with the prosecution's theory that my client fired a gun. You heard my client had no gun shot residue on his hands approximately twelve hours after the shooting. I submit to you that proves he didn't fire the gun. The prosecution will argue he washed his hands to get rid of the residue. Let's think about that logic. The prosecution would have you believe that my client was smart enough to know to wash his hands to get rid of the gunshot residue, but he forgot to dispose of the gun. The prosecution's logic is inconsistent.

"Let's talk about the lack of evidence. That is the most glaring problem with this case. Other than the gun in my client's car, there is no physical evidence tying my client to the crime. There are no fingerprints, hair samples, or DNA samples tying my client to the crime. No one ever saw my client at the Edison Home after he was asked to leave by the police. My client allowed his house and vehicles to be searched, and he answered the policemen's' questions. He cooperated with the police, and he acted like an innocent man—he was angry when he realized someone had planted the murder weapon in his vehicle. Just like he was angry when the prosecutor told you lies in his closing argument."

Spere jumped up. "Objection."

Judge Stalman said, "Sustained."

Ray walked over to Dallas and stood behind him. "It looked bad when the murder weapon was found in my client's car. Just like it looks bad with my client bound and gagged. But ladies and gentlemen, the truth of this trial can't be gagged. The truth will shine during your deliberations."

Ray looked up at Judge Stalman and loudly announced, "The defense rests, Your Honor."

Chapter 24

Friday morning, 11:48 a.m.

Judge Stalman watched the last juror go into the jury room and the head bailiff shut the door behind them. He looked back at Spere and Ray as he announced, "We are in recess until the jury returns with a verdict."

The judge stood up and the head bailiff said, "All rise." After the judge walked off the bench and into his chambers, everyone relaxed. Dallas looked at Ray and mumbled something through the handkerchief. Ray gave him a quizzical look and Dallas gave him a thumbs up sign with his left hand. Ray nodded and smiled.

The assistant bailiff stepped forward and instructed Dallas to step to the side of the counsel table. Everyone in the courtroom watched as he was unchained and ungagged. Reporters were writing furiously in their note pads, and everyone listened for Dallas's first words.

"Can I have some water?" Dallas asked politely.

The head bailiff motioned toward the holding cell, and Dallas began walking back to it. As he walked by Ray, he whispered, "Thanks. I know you did your best."
Ray lied, "I'm sure the jury will see it our way."

Everyone in the courtroom watched Dallas walk slowly back to the holding cell. As Dallas rounded the corner of the courtroom and walked down the hallway, he asked his bailiff escort, "What do you think?"

The head bailiff shrugged. "Could go either way. You didn't help yourself slamming the table." Dallas looked down and muttered, "I know."

Dallas entered the holding cell and the head bailiff locked the door behind him. The head bailiff motioned toward the stainless bench and said, "They brought you over some lunch. You've got to stay here until they have a verdict."

The head bailiff walked down the hall and left Dallas with his lunch. Dallas looked over at the yellow lunch tray, hoping for something different. But it was Friday, so that meant fish sticks, and macaroni and cheese, with vinegar flavored coleslaw, and milk to drink. He picked up a fish stick and bit off the end. It was cold and stiff, but he choked it down. He opened up his milk carton and took a swig of the warm milk. It took a second for his taste buds to tell him the milk was spoiled. He lunged at the commode and puked everything back up.

** ** ** ** **

Ray walked out of the courtroom and saw Helen and his girls. Beth and Julie ran over and gave him a hug. Beth squealed, "Daddy, you did great, and your suit is so much better than the prosecutor's blue blazer and khakis. Where'd you get that cool tie?"

Ray looked down and touched his yellow tie as he tried to remember. "I think I got it at Macy's last summer."

Beth said, "It's way cool."

The girls released their hug and stepped back. Helen had drifted up closer, but she wasn't saying anything. Julie asked, "So Dad, you really think one of his ex-girlfriends shot him?"

Ray focused on Julie. "I think so, honey. But what matters is what the jury thinks."

Beth asked, "What do you think he did to his ex-lover

to make her so mad she killed him?"

Ray forced a smile. "I'm not a woman; I don't know what it'd take. Why don't you ask your mom?"

Both of the girls looked at Helen, and her face flushed. She shrugged and said dryly, "I have no idea."

Ray put his arms around his girls and pulled them close. "Juries usually take a long time on murder cases. There's no need for you to hang around here. I'll call you when we have a verdict."

** ** ** ** **

Helen gave Ray a nasty look as she turned around and walked to the stairs without the girls. She heard the girls say goodbye to Ray and run to catch up to her. They started talking about which movie they wanted to see. Helen was seething at Ray's remark to her. She never told the girls about her affair with Bryce, but who knows what other kids had told them at school. As Helen ground her teeth, she conceded it could've been a lot worse.

If Ray had tried to talk about her in closing argument, she had planned to stay there with the girls and start crying. She was going to create a scene and make sure all of the reporters saw how devastated she was that her ex-husband would stoop so low. She was going to make sure the girls knew she was humiliated.

Fortunately, Ray hadn't tried to expose her as the real murderer. At least not yet. Maybe he was holding that in his back pocket to use if his client was convicted. He could file a motion for new trial and allege newly discovered evidence. The press would have a field day with it, and she'd have her name in the headlines and someone would remind the press of her prior affair with Bryce. No, she wasn't out of the woods yet.

** ** ** ** **

As his girls walked away, Ray felt very tired. He walked over to a well-worn wooden bench and sat down. He could smell his body odor from the last two days. It was part sweat, part jail floor essence, and part stress-produced secretions. Unfortunately, he couldn't leave the courthouse for a shower. He walked over to the bathroom and washed his face and gargled with tap water.

He walked back out to the bench and pulled out his cell phone. He hit the speed dial for Doug, who answered on the second ring.

"Hey, Ray. What's happening?"

"The jury went out a few minutes ago."

"What do you think?"

"It could go either way."

Ray was quiet for a few seconds, and Doug didn't volunteer anything. Finally, Ray asked, "Where's Amber?"

Doug answered quietly, "The doctor finished the procedure five minutes ago. The doctor is keeping her in the recovery room for an hour to make sure there's no excess bleeding."

Ray hung up the phone, and a tear rolled down his cheek.

** ** ** ** **

Spere's wife, Ethel, shut his office door, seething with anger. She asked angrily, "What the hell went on at the sidebar about your black eye? What did that defense lawyer say about me?"

Spere put his index finger to his lips. Ethel growled, "Don't shush me."

Spere gave up having a private conversation behind his closed door without his secretary listening. "Harrison wanted to throw off my timing, so he brought up a rumor of you giving me a black eye."

Ethel stepped forward and squeezed his arms as she asked desperately, "Why didn't you do something?"

Spere jerked his arms away. "I did. I objected, and the judge ruled in my favor. The jury never heard it."

Ethel's voice cracked as she whispered, "Well, the court reporter told one of her girlfriends in the clerk's office, and it's all around the courthouse. Everyone in my office is looking at me strangely."

Spere walked behind his desk and sat down. He leaned back in his chair and watched his wife standing next to the closed door, biting her fingernails. After a few seconds of silence, he said quietly, "Maybe you should resign and go to counseling."

She snapped her head toward Spere and said, "I don't need counseling, and I will not let you control me by making me quit my job."

** ** ** ** **

Judge Stalman took off his robe and paced around his chambers, cracking his knuckles, and obsessing over Ray's comments about gagging the truth. He couldn't let that go unchallenged, or the other lawyers wouldn't respect him. He was going to do a follow-up letter to the Florida Bar about Ray's closing argument. A DUI arrest and trying to embarrass a trial judge within a twelve hour period—that ought to get the Bar's attention.

Judge Stalman walked over to his small refrigerator and grabbed a bottle of Starbucks double cappuccino. He sat down in his overstuffed burgundy desk chair and took a drink of the potent mixture. He leaned back in his chair and tried to relax, but he was still agitated over Ray's antics. The more he thought about it, the madder he got. He decided to kill some time with light office work while the jury deliberated.

He flipped through his bills and got depressed. He sat up and looked at his full incoming box. There were boring memos from court administration and the chief judge of the circuit. However, a pink envelope caught his attention.

It was addressed to him and marked personal and confidential in bold letters. He opened the envelope and immediately smelled the perfume. He unfolded the letter and saw cursive handwriting in blue ink on pink stationary. The wide curves of the letters seemed to indicate a woman's hand. He pulled it closer and read:

Dear Judge Stalman,
It was a pleasure appearing in your courtroom this week. I left my address and work number with your judicial assistant in case of problems with my travel voucher. But this letter is meant for your eyes only. I will be at the FDLE lab working all of next week, but I'll be in a seminar next weekend in Miami. It would be nice if you could meet me there. My cell number is 813.555.2323.
Joyce Napier

Judge Stalman smiled and dialed his wife at home. She

answered cheerily, "Hello."

Judge Stalman responded sweetly, "Hi honey, how are you?"

"I'm doing fine. How's the trial going?"

"The jury's been deliberating for about ten minutes. I don't know how long they'll deliberate; this case is a close one."

"Do you want me to make dinner, or do you want to eat out?"

Judge Stalman knew his wife hated to cook. "We can eat out. By the way, I got a call from an old college buddy that's gonna be in Miami next weekend fishing with his son. Do you mind if I go over Saturday and stay for the weekend?"

"No, that's fine honey. I've got the Junior League fundraiser on Saturday anyway."

Chapter 25

Friday afternoon, 5:12 p.m.

"All rise. The Honorable Gary Stalman is presiding over this court."

Judge Stalman walked in and sat down. He glanced around the courtroom, looking for any quick sitters. He was ready to nail someone with a full courtroom. After glancing around he realized everyone had learned his tricks, so he said politely, "You may be seated."

After everyone sat down and the courtroom quieted down, Judge Stalman said somberly, "We have a verdict."

Judge Stalman looked at Dallas, who had been re-gagged and bound. "I don't want any further reaction from you, Mr. Kelley. If you continue to disrupt my courtroom, you will be tased. Do I make myself clear?"

Dallas nodded meekly.

Judge Stalman looked up at the large number of spectators in the courtroom. "I don't want any reaction from the audience, or I'll find you in contempt." Judge Stalman hesitated to let his warning sink in and then looked at his head bailiff. "Bring in the jury."

Everyone stood up in the courtroom as the jurors walked in, and they stared at all of the spectators looking at them.

After the last one came out of the jury room, Judge Stalman said, "Everyone may be seated."

Judge Stalman looked at a middle-aged female juror on the second row, who was holding a paper, and asked, "Mrs. Murray, it looks like you've been elected foreperson. Do you have a verdict?"

Mrs. Murray stood up and said shakily, "Yes we do, Your Honor."

"Please give it to the bailiff."

The head bailiff stepped forward, took the verdict, and walked it to the judge. Judge Stalman reached over the bench for it. He looked at it for five seconds, looked to his left, and passed the verdict to his matronly clerk. "Madame clerk, would you publish the verdict?"

The clerk slowly grasped the verdict like it was a snake and took another five seconds to examine it while everyone in the courtroom searched her face for a clue. Both the judge and clerk had perfect poker faces, and the wait was becoming unbearable. Finally, the clerk spoke, "We, the jury, find the defendant not guilty."

The courtroom erupted in noise, and the judge screamed for order. Dallas collapsed into his chair, tears running down his cheek. Ray sat down next to him and hugged him. The noise finally settled down, and Judge Stalman bellowed, "Bailiff, release the defendant."

Dallas stood up and stepped next to the counsel table. The courtroom was silent as the locks were undone first, and then the handkerchiefs. Dallas rubbed his wrists and took a deep breath as Judge Stalman said, "You have been found not guilty by a jury of your peers, so I order you released from custody. This court is adjourned."

Judge Stalman slammed the gavel down. As he walked off the bench, he gave Ray a dirty look.

Dallas embraced Ray and whispered in his ear, "I owe you my life. Thanks."

Ray was elated. "You're welcome."

Dallas looked Ray in the eyes. "Come celebrate with me.

I haven't had anything to drink since I've been in."

Ray smiled and said, "I'll pass. I need to dry out a little bit."

Dallas smiled back. "Yeah, right."

Dallas turned toward the audience and pumped his fist. His supporters swarmed forward and pulled him out of courtroom to cheers. Ray looked over at the jury and half of them were crying while the other half smiled. Ray mouthed a thank you and turned to walk through the crowd. The head bailiff motioned for the jury to follow him and told them they'd be escorted out the rear exit of the courtroom.

Ray received many handshakes and congratulations as he walked out of the courtroom. He walked through the courtroom's outer door and was met by the shining lights of the TV cameras. A young brunette reporter stuck a microphone in his face and asked, "What's your reaction to the verdict?"

Ray scratched his chin as he contemplated his sound bite. "The jury was courageous. They thoughtfully analyzed the evidence and realized Dallas wasn't the killer. The police and prosecutors made mistakes investigating this murder. If they continue their investigation, maybe they can find the woman that killed Bryce Cervante."

About the Author

John D. Mills is a fifth generation native of Ft. Myers, Florida. He grew up fishing the waters of Pine Island Sound and it's still his favorite hobby. He graduated from Mercer University in Macon, Georgia with a BBA in Finance and worked for Lee County Bank in Ft. Myers for five months. He returned to Macon and graduated from Mercer's law school in 1989.

He started his legal career as a prosecutor for the State Attorney's Office in Ft. Myers. In 1990, he began his private practice concentrating in Divorce and Criminal Defense.

Made in the USA
Coppell, TX
28 August 2021

61377383R00152